What's his Passion?

CLIMBING THE
SAVAGE MOUNTAIN

T.A. CHASE

Climbing the Savage Mountain
ISBN # 978-1-78430-821-6
©Copyright T.A. Chase 2015
Cover Art by Posh Gosh ©Copyright October 2015
Interior text design by Claire Siemaszkiewicz
Pride Publishing

Published in 2015 by Pride Publishing, Newland House, The Point, Weaver Road, Lincoln, LN6 3QN, United Kingdom.

Pride Publishing is a subsidiary of Totally Entwined Group Limited.

CLIMBING THE SAVAGE MOUNTAIN

Dedication

To Sue, my awesome editor who made sure I got the
climbing components right along with everything else.
To Jackie Nacht: sprinting with you is such fun. Thank
you so much.

Author's Note

Climbing the Savage Mountain was written before the
tragic earthquake and avalanche in Nepal. My
thoughts and prayers go out to all the climbers,
Sherpas and people of Nepal who lost loved ones.

Also, this story was written before the Supreme Court
decision making marriage equality legal in all fifty
states.

Pride Publishing books by T.A. Chase:

Out of Light into Darkness
From Slavery to Freedom
The Vanguard
Two for One
Where the Devil Dances
Stealing Life

The Four Horsemen
Pestilence
War
Famine
Death

The Beasor Chronicles
Gypsies
Tramps

Home
No Going Home
Home of His Own
Wishing for a Home
Leaving Home
Home Sweet Home

Every Shattered Dream
Part One
Part Two
Part Three
Part Four
Part Five

Rags to Riches Volume One
Remove the Empty Spaces
Close the Distance

Rags to Riches Volume Two
Following His Footsteps
Anywhere Tequila Flows

Rags to Riches Volume Three
Walking in the Rain
Barefoot Dancing

Delarosa Secrets
Borderline
Snap Decision
Cold Truth

The Blood and Thorn Ranch
Bulls and Blood

What's his Passion?
Mountains to Climb
Climbing the Savage Mountain

Anthologies:
Unconventional at Best: Ninja Cupcakes
Unconventional in Atlanta: His Last Client
An Unconventional Chicago: No Bravery
Semper Fidelis: Always Ready
Aim High: Possibilities

Part One

Mount Everest

The first question you will ask and which I must try to answer is this, 'what is the use of climbing Mount Everest?' and my answer at once must be, 'it is no use.' There is not the slightest prospect of gain whatsoever. Oh, we might learn a little about the behavior of the human body at high altitudes, and possibly medical men may turn our observation to some account for the purpose of aviation. But otherwise nothing will come of it. We shall not bring back a single bit of gold or silver, not a gem, nor any coal or iron. We shall not find a single foot of earth that can be planted with crops to raise food. It's no use. So, if you cannot understand that there is something in man which responds to the challenge of this mountain and goes out to meet it, that the struggle is the struggle of life itself upward and forever upward, then you won't see why we go. What we get from this adventure is just sheer joy. And joy is, after all, the end of life. We do not live to eat and make money. We eat and make money to be able to live. That is what life means and what life is for.

– George Mallory

Chapter One

My mind is in a state of constant rebellion. I believe that will always be so.

— George Mallory

Toby let the door slam behind him as he entered his house. "Jensen? Are you here?"

No answer and Toby's heart started to race. He tossed his keys in the bowl on the table in the foyer before he took off his jacket. Even a year later, he always panicked when he came home and Jensen wasn't around. One would think he'd be over worrying that Jensen would leave him again.

Last year when Jensen Brockhoff had shown up out of the blue after disappearing for six years, Toby had convinced himself to forgive him and give Jensen another chance. Hell, Jensen had promised he'd never leave Toby again, and for the most part, Toby believed him. Yet there was just a small piece of his heart that figured Jensen's wanderlust would kick in, and Toby would come home to an empty house with only a note explaining where Jensen had gone.

"Jensen?" he called again, picking up his briefcase before stalking down the hallway toward the back of the house.

Sometimes Jensen would be in the kitchen, wearing headphones while he cooked their supper. Toby had told him a hundred times just to plug his iPod into the stereo system that ran through the entire house, but Jensen said he liked feeling surrounded by the music — whatever that meant.

He left his briefcase in his study then walked into the kitchen. No Jensen. Toby took a deep breath, trying very hard not to start thinking bad things. He'd known something had been bothering Jensen the past week or so, but when Toby had asked him about it, he just brushed it off as mid-winter blues. He'd let it go because he'd been swamped at work.

Next time don't let him distract you. Keep at him until he tells you what's wrong. He'll leave if you don't get him to talk.

Toby stripped off his tie then unbuttoned the top two buttons on his shirt. He'd hung his suit coat on the banister, so he'd remember to take it upstairs later. After flinging the tie on the island counter, Toby braced his hands on the edge of the granite, closed his eyes and took two deep calming breathes.

"Hey man, I didn't hear you come in. Been home long?"

Jumping slightly, Toby whirled around to watch as Jensen strolled in from the back yard, a pair of tongs in his hand. His headphones were hanging around his neck, which Toby took to mean he really hadn't heard him yelling or the car pulling into the driveway.

Jensen set the tongs near the sink before coming over to Toby. He encircled Toby's waist then pulled him tight against his body. Their mouths met and Toby sighed as all the tension he'd been feeling drained from him. He buried his hands in Jensen's long hair, twisting his fingers to keep his lover still while he bit his bottom lip. Toby swept his tongue in when Jensen opened for him.

"Hmm..." he hummed, tasting something spicy as he kissed him. When they broke apart, he grinned. "Are we having chips and salsa along with our steaks tonight?"

"I might have already sampled the salsa." Jensen winked. "Have to make sure it's just spicy enough for my guy."

Toby rolled his eyes, but didn't try to move away when Jensen kissed him again. This was one of the things he'd grown to love now that Jensen was back and they were living together. It was something they hadn't had when they were dating the first time. It had been more like friends with benefits, though Toby had always wanted more. Jensen had disappeared before Toby was able to say anything.

He whimpered when Jensen slid his hands to get two handfuls of his ass and squeezed. When Toby let his head drop back, Jensen licked a trail from the corner of his lips down to the soft skin at the base of his throat. Toby shuddered at the thought of wearing a mark like that as a sign that he belonged to Jensen. Keeping his hands in Jensen's hair, Toby pressed his mouth a little tighter to his skin, wanting it more than he could ever voice.

Finally, Jensen exerted enough pressure to break free of Toby's hold on him. He stepped back a few inches and smiled. "I need to go check the steaks. Why don't you grab the salad out of the fridge? The table's set and I made some apple cider for us."

"Can I go change first?" He gestured to his dress clothes then to the ripped jeans and long sleeve sweater Jensen wore. "Someone's a little more comfortable than I am."

Jensen chuckled. "Go ahead, man. Wouldn't want you to get your work clothes dirty. I can finish getting everything on the table."

"Thanks." Toby swooped in for another kiss before he dashed toward the back staircase. "I'll be right back down."

"You better be, or I'm going to skip the steak and eat the chocolate cake I baked for you."

Toby skidded to a halt at the foot of the stairs. He turned to eye Jensen. "What's going on? Why did you bake me a cake? Are you leaving again?"

Jensen waved his questions away. "We'll talk after dinner. I also don't want the meat to get burned. So go."

As much as Toby loved Jensen's chocolate cake, the excitement at the possibility of eating it had dulled. Knowing that it had been cooked to soften a coming blow didn't make Toby want to race upstairs anymore. He leaned against the wall and stared at Jensen who puttered around the kitchen, avoiding his gaze.

"Jensen? Come on, talk to me. Are you going on another climbing trip?"

He didn't really like the trips Jensen took to climb some of the world's most dangerous mountains, but he'd never tried to stop him. Toby understood that it was how Jensen coped with the stress of the world around him. Jensen had tried to deal with drugs and alcohol and all that had done was make him a recovering addict.

At least with climbing, he was doing something healthy. Toby silently amended that. The kind of high altitude expeditions Jensen went on would have him leave excited and happy to go on the journey, and return to Toby wasted away from the toll conquering the mountain had taken on him.

Toby didn't like seeing Jensen diminished in any way, and he wasn't a hundred percent sure climbing was the best thing for Jensen. It was almost as though he replaced one addiction with another and any of them could kill him if he wasn't careful.

"Toby. Please, go change and come back down to eat. I told you. We'll talk about it after dinner."

Jensen looked up then and Toby saw the almost feverish glow in his lover's eyes—a glow that caused his heart to sink. Jensen was leaving again, and Toby didn't know if he could stand it one more time.

He trudged up the stairs to their bedroom where he quickly changed. His dress shirt went in the pile for the dry cleaners, along with his pants. His shoes were lined up neatly with the others at the bottom of the closet, socks and undershirt tossed into the hamper.

Toby dug out his favorite pair of ripped jeans and the Wyoming sweatshirt he'd stolen from Jensen. Once he got those on, he tugged on a pair of thick socks before heading back down to where Jensen waited for him. He tried to summon a smile for his lover when he stepped into the dining room, but he didn't have one to give.

"Sit and eat." Jensen motioned to his usual spot at the table. "I already poured you some cider."

Toby frowned. "You managed to do all this after working at the gym today? You know you didn't have to go to all this trouble. I could've picked something up on the way home."

Jensen shook his head. "Don't worry about it, Toby. I don't mind cooking. It helps unclutter my mind."

Like climbing, Jensen had discovered an affinity for cooking and he was quite good at it. Toby would never complain about returning from work to find a home-cooked meal on the table waiting for him. He just didn't want it to be because Jensen was trying to figure out how to tell him he was leaving.

Gripping his knife until his knuckles turned white, Toby stared at Jensen. "Please tell me. You know the waiting makes it worse. How long will you be gone this time?"

Sighing, Jensen set his fork down before meeting Toby's gaze. "Do you remember me telling you that Cat, Jigger and I had planned on climbing Everest last year?"

Toby nodded even while his heart sank. Everest. One of two mountains still on Jensen's bucket list. He took a quick swallow of cider, wishing it were beer instead before he motioned for Jensen to continue.

"We couldn't last year because the climbing season was suspended after all those Sherpas were killed and the rest went on strike. You can't climb Everest without Sherpas to help you. I don't care what anyone says. Those men are mountain gods. I wouldn't go on any expedition to Everest that didn't use them." Jensen stabbed at his steak, his expression fierce.

"I remember you telling me about the avalanche and that it was the deadliest single day incident on the mountain ever—even worse than the nineteen-ninety-six storm." Toby held back the shudder threatening to take over his body at the thought of Jensen being up on that mountain when the storms started rolling in.

"Yeah. So they canceled the season and we couldn't go. Well, Jigger called this morning and said that we got our permit and we're going this year." He was practically bouncing in his chair. "I'm going to fly out to Wyoming at the end of February so we can get in some real climbs and train together. We're flying into Katmandu around the end of March. We need to get to Base Camp in April."

"February?"

It was the second week of January. He should be glad he'd had Jensen around for Christmas and New Year's.

"Yeah. I'm sorry. I would've let you know sooner, but we weren't sure we'd get another permit. The climbing season starts in March, but we decided to try and get there for the optimal time to summit, which is May." Jensen took a deep breath and Toby could see him visibly reining in his excitement.

He didn't move when Jensen reached across the table to take his hand with his own. Toby looked into Jensen's hazel eyes and saw the spark that had always attracted him to Jensen. For the most part nowadays, it was there because of him. Yet Toby knew that the only other thing that could make Jensen shine like that was climbing.

"When will you be back?"

Toby tried to keep his hold on Jensen light, as though he were sheltering baby chicks in his hands. He was exhausted from worrying about clinging to Jensen, afraid that if he became too needy, Jensen wouldn't come back from one of his climbs. That he'd run away again like he did seven years ago.

"By the end of May or beginning of June — no later. I'll go back to Wyoming with Jigger and Cat to make sure they're okay then I'll come straight back here." Jensen's grip on Toby's hand tightened and Toby gritted his teeth. "I've been dreaming about Everest since I first started climbing."

"You told me that. You'll be able to cross it off your bucket list if you summit, right?" he asked, hoping it wouldn't turn into something Jensen wanted to do all the time.

"Yep. *When* we summit. There's no doubt the three of us are going to make it all the way up to the top. I don't plan on spending all that money and traveling that far not to conquer that mountain." Jensen's grin held supreme confidence.

Shifting in his seat, Toby tugged his hand free then reached down to adjust his cock in his jeans. Jensen leaned back in his chair with a smirk on his face. The ass knew exactly what he was doing to Toby.

"After Everest, you'll have only one more mountain to summit, then you can focus on something else," Toby commented, not willing to acknowledge the erection he was sporting. That was something they could both address after dinner.

"Yeah. K2, a bitch of a piece of wind-scarred rock. A lot of people think Everest is the pinnacle of climbing, but not me. To summit K2, you need balls and guts. I think it'll be technically more difficult than Everest as well." Jensen rubbed his chin. "I have to call Cat and Jigger. One of the guys we climb with a lot has applied for a permit to climb one of the routes on that mountain. I need to find out if he's heard from the Pakistani government yet."

Toby watched as Jensen drifted off, obviously starting to make a checklist for his K2 climb. He stretched to grab a roll then tossed it at Jensen, hitting him smack in the face. Jensen jerked and glared at him.

"What the hell was that for?" Jensen snatched the bread off the floor then dropped it on the table. "Are you trying to start a food fight?"

"No. Don't get ahead of yourself. You have a more recent climb to train and plan for. You don't need to be figuring out the logistics on the K2 trip yet." Toby didn't want him to go on *either* expedition, yet he didn't feel like he could ask Jensen to stay home, not when he was so close to reaching his ultimate goal.

Jensen shook his entire body as though he were getting rid of everything except what was going on around him at that moment. After taking a sip of his cider, he smiled at Toby.

"How was work?"

Toby shrugged. "Crazy. You would think someone flipped a switch somewhere. Clients want to buy—or sell—and I'm trying to convince them all not do to a fire sale. The markets have been relatively steady the past couple of months. I guess people think that something bad is about to happen and they want to get out before it does. Or some of them want to see how much money they can make from other people's panic."

"Man, I don't miss those days. I'd usually be calling my dealer about one in the afternoon and get him to make a delivery. Plus the fifth of whiskey I kept in my bottom desk drawer would be empty by the time I left work." Jensen rocked back on the hind legs of the chair, arms folded over his chest.

"Seriously? I guess I didn't know dealers made house calls. Of course, I wasn't into drugs that much. Did some once in a while when we went clubbing, but never got hooked." He took a bite of his steak that had gotten cold while they talked.

Jensen let his chair fall back to the floor. "Yeah. I always wanted to tell you not to do any of that shit when we went out because I was so afraid you'd get caught up in it like me. I was happy when it seemed like you were only a recreational user."

"I stopped doing even that when you disappeared," Toby confessed. "I didn't go out much for a while after that. I tended to drink my sorrows, not drug myself into a stupor."

"I'm sorry," Jensen apologized for the millionth time.

He held up his hand. "Stop apologizing. I forgave you when you agreed to move in with me."

Chapter Two

To struggle and to understand. Never the last without the first. That is the law.

— George Mallory

That might have been true, but Jensen felt as if he could never apologize enough for the hurt he'd caused Toby when he ran away. *If I'm so sorry about it, why do I keep leaving?* He kept waiting for Toby to ask him that every time he headed out on another climbing trip. Yet Toby never questioned him, just let Jensen take off for months on end and always welcomed him back with open arms.

How much longer can I expect him to wait around? At some point, he's going to realize this isn't the perfect relationship I'd promised him we'd have.

He dropped his gaze to the empty plate in front of him. Jensen clenched his hands, fighting the need for a drink of whiskey or scotch — anything that would dull the emotions swirling around in his head. But he didn't drink anymore and there wasn't any alcohol in the house.

Toby had stopped drinking as well when he'd learned about Jensen's addiction, just another sign of how much Toby loved him. He felt like an ass because he was so excited to finally be able to climb Everest and he could see how much Toby wanted to be happy for him, but the thought of Jensen being gone for so long was apparently not something Toby wanted to dwell on.

After jumping to his feet, Jensen carried their plates into the kitchen then grabbed the cake off the counter. He'd baked it earlier that day after getting Jigger's call about the trip. In the back of his mind, he must have wanted to soften the blow because he knew Toby wasn't going to be happy about it.

When he got back to the dining room, Toby was standing by the large bay window that overlooked their backyard. He'd rested one hand on the window frame and was rubbing his neck with the other. Tension rolled off him, making Jensen wish for the hundredth time that he wasn't a completely selfish asshole who wasn't going to ask Toby to be patient two more times.

"How big do you want your piece?" Jensen interjected a hint of joviality into his voice. He held the knife poised over the cake.

Toby glanced over his shoulder at him and shrugged. "I'm not really hungry for cake right now. Maybe we could have some later."

"Okay. Did you want to go take a shower? Or I thought we could go for a run later," he suggested.

"A run would be nice." Toby inhaled deeply and squared his shoulders before turning to face Jensen. "Tell me more about Everest. You said you're flying into Katmandu? That's in Nepal, right?"

Toby was trying and Jensen had to honor his attempt. He put the cake away then got the pitcher of cider from the fridge. After refilling their glasses, he took Toby's hand and led him into the living room where he got Toby settled on the couch. Jensen started a fire in the fireplace before joining his lover.

He entwined their fingers together, rubbing his thumb over Toby's knuckles as he thought about what he could say to convince Toby to be excited about the whole situation. Finally, he just decided to talk. Maybe something in his words would spark an emotion in Toby.

"Yeah. It's the capital of Nepal. We fly in there then head to Lukla where we'll trek up to Everest Base Camp. The company we're going through plans expeditions up the Southeast Face. The North Col, which is on the Chinese side, is a technically more difficult climb, but none of us want to deal with the bullshit that China's government hands out from time to time. It's easier to go through Nepal." Jensen shrugged.

Toby looked interested, though Jensen wasn't entirely sure if he really felt that way or was simply trying to be nice.

"Why Everest?" Toby asked. "Whenever I hear people talk about something on their bucket list — or the ultimate dream — a lot of them say climbing Everest. What makes Everest such a goal?"

Jensen scrubbed his hand over his hair as he tried to think about how to explain how he felt whenever he imagined climbing Everest. "I don't know about other people, though for most of them, Everest might seem like the biggest insurmountable obstacle they can think of. And to be able to say they got to the summit ends up putting them in a rare class of people who have faced a challenge and defeated it."

Toby nodded. "I guess that makes sense, but why do *you* want to climb it? I know that it's only number two on your list. K2 is the one you really want to conquer. Why not focus on that one instead of risking everything on Everest?"

Jensen met Toby's gaze and said, "If I can summit Everest, I have no doubt that I'll get to the summit of K2."

"So Everest is just a litmus test as to your ability to climb big mountains? What happens if you end up getting injured while trying it? Will that convince you that you can't do it or will it strengthen your resolve to try again?" Toby clenched his hands.

He winced at the pressure Toby exerted on his fingers. Jensen cupped Toby's face in his free hand.

"Nothing will happen to me on this trip. I promise."

Toby jerked away from him then shot to his feet. He started pacing while Jensen watched. "Don't promise me something like that, Jensen. You're a good climber. I know that. Hell, Cat and Jigger tell me that all the time. You're a natural. One of the best they've seen in years. I know that means jack shit when you're up on that godforsaken piece of rock and a storm rolls in."

Jensen opened his mouth then snapped it shut when Toby whirled on him. He saw the fear in Toby's eyes and he rushed to him, wrapping his arms around his lover to hold him close. He pressed his mouth to Toby's ear and whispered, "I promise to never make light of your fears. I'm sorry. I guess I didn't realize how scared you were about me going."

"It's not just Everest, Jensen," Toby confessed. "It's every time you walk out that door on a trip. I'm left here, wondering if you're going to come home. So far you've done it, but what if something keeps you from coming back to me?"

As much as he wanted to say that the only way he wouldn't be coming back to Toby was if he were dead, Jensen knew it wasn't the right thing to say. It certainly wouldn't reassure Toby at all.

"I know you're afraid I'll decide to keep wandering." He stepped back to stare down at Toby. "I can make you this vow, Toby, and this one I *do* have control over. I will *always* come back to you. I wasn't strong enough to face you when I ran away before. I didn't trust in how much you cared for me. We both know I should've come to you and told you about my addictions and my problems."

"Damn straight you should've. How can I help you when I don't know what's wrong?" Toby encircled Jensen's waist, resting his head on Jensen's chest.

Jensen kissed the top of Toby's head. "Do you really feel like talking about my trip right now? Why don't we go for a run then when we get back, we can take a shower?"

Tension eased from Toby's shoulders and Jensen realized it was just a reprieve from the complications of him going away. Yet he didn't want to talk about it right then. He wanted to spend time with the man he loved and soak up all the good times, so he had something to cling to when he was on the side of Everest, praying to God to keep him safe.

"All right. Thank God, the roads are clear. That storm we had two days ago dumped a lot of snow, but looks like the road commission got the trucks out." Toby eased away, but took his hand and led him toward the stairs. He scooped up his suit coat.

"If you set out your clothes, I'll drop them off at the dry cleaners tomorrow on my way to the gym," Jensen told Toby as they went into their room to change.

"Thanks. Since I forgot to take them last week, I'm running low on shirts." Toby chuckled. "How do you feel about being the house husband while I go to work every day?"

Jensen dug through their dresser, pulling out two pairs of running tights and two long sleeved sweatshirts for them. "To be honest, I thought I'd hate it," he confessed as he stripped. "Before I left, I was always busy with work, going out or doing a hundred other things. Even after rehab, I kept myself moving and doing odd jobs while waiting for my next climb. But I like doing stuff for you, whether it's taking care of your dry cleaning or cooking dinner. There's so many things to do around the house."

Toby removed his jeans, distracting Jensen when he bent over and Jensen found himself staring at Toby's perfect ass. After reaching over, Jensen pinched him and Toby squeaked. He burst out laughing when Toby glared at him while rubbing his abused flesh.

"What the hell was that for?"

"Couldn't resist. You stuck it out there." He wiggled his eyebrows and Toby rolled his eyes.

"Sometimes I think you're channeling a twelve year old." Toby dressed quickly, as though he didn't want Jensen to get any more ideas.

Frowning, Jensen adjusted his cock in the jockstrap he'd put on. *Christ!* He hoped the cold air would take care of the problem because it was a bitch running with a hard-on. He dressed then put on his running shoes. They jogged down the stairs before heading outside.

They stretched and Jensen wanted to discuss his training schedule with Toby, but he'd said they wouldn't talk about Everest for now. There would be enough conversation as the weeks progressed and he didn't want Toby to end up hating the idea of him going. Because if Toby ever asked him not to go, Jensen would seriously have to consider doing what Toby wanted. It would always bug him not to have gone to Everest when the opportunity presented itself, but if Toby was that scared about him going, he would stay home.

"Ready?" Toby smiled at him.

"Yes." Jensen gestured for Toby to take the lead. He'd follow that round, firm butt anywhere.

Neither of them were talkers while they ran. They'd discovered they were evenly matched in stride and pace. Both of them enjoyed running. Toby had told him once that it helped him clear his mind from all the shit he dealt with during the day at work. For Jensen, it helped him organize his thoughts, but also it helped build up his lung capacity and stamina. It was just a small part of his training regime. When he got to Wyoming, they'd do several fourteen thousand feet climbs to help get him as used to higher altitudes as he could get before he left for Nepal.

Jackie, their neighbor, waved to them when they passed her house. Jensen waved back, smiling at the sight of her two little kids playing in the front yard. On his days off, he would wander down and entertain them for a while so that Jackie could have some time to herself. Jensen liked kids. He studied Toby's back as they continued along their street.

They'd never discussed kids — or really anything that felt like a future. Was that because Toby still wasn't convinced Jensen would stay? Considering what he'd said earlier, Jensen had a feeling that was it. Would Toby be interested in adopting a child — or two? It wasn't as if they didn't have the money to support kids. Jensen had invested most of his earnings and, even with all of the climbing trips, he still had a very substantial nest egg.

Toby could still go into the city every day for work, and Jensen would be more than happy to be a stay-at-home dad. Or if Toby wanted to stay home with the kids, they could both be that. There wasn't a written law anywhere that at least one of them — or both of them — had to work.

He stumbled over a crack in the sidewalk and pin wheeled his arms to keep from falling flat on his face. "Fuck!" He cringed when Toby glanced back at him and smirked.

"Head in the clouds, Brockhoff?" Then Toby pursed his lips for a second. "I guess that might be possible. How high is Everest? Your head is probably at least that high up in the sky, huh?"

"The summit is twenty-nine thousand twenty-eight feet in the air," he muttered. "But that wasn't what I was thinking about."

Looking surprised, Toby slowed so that they were running side by side. "No? What had you so distracted then? I haven't seen you take a wrong step like that since we started running together."

"Do you want to have kids?" Jensen blurted then blushed, not really wanting to have asked that.

Toby halted, forcing Jensen to do the same. Giving him a narrow-eyed stare, Toby inquired, "Where did that come from?"

Jensen heaved a sigh before waving his hand back in the direction they'd just come from. "I saw Jackie and her kids outside and I got to wondering if you liked kids. I realized we'd never discussed them before. Then I got thinking about whether you wanted some or not. We have more than enough money to be able to support them, and if you wanted to keep working, I'd be more than happy to stay home with them."

He was babbling and Toby stared at him as though he'd grown three new heads or four arms all of a sudden. Jensen dropped his gaze to the concrete in front of him and stubbed his toe on it.

"Never mind. It's not important. I just got thinking about it then my mouth took over from my brain and dumped the question on you." He motioned ahead of them. "Let's get moving again. It's fucking cold out here."

Toby startled him by stepping up to him then rising up on his toes to press a kiss to his lips. When he tilted his head in a silent question, Toby grinned.

"I'd love to have a family with you, but I think we should shelve the discussion until after you're done with your climbing trips. It's not fair for a child to have his — or her — parent disappear for months at a time, unless said parent is in the military," Toby qualified.

Excitement shot through Jensen and he couldn't help grabbing Toby and whirling him around in a big circle. Toby looked at him as though he couldn't figure out exactly what Jensen had taken to make him react that way.

He set Toby down and grinned. "You're right. It wouldn't be fair to you or the kids if I took off for months at a time, doing things that were fun for me. That's selfish and I'm not that kind of guy anymore."

"Don't you think we should talk about maybe getting married before we discuss adding children to the mix?"

"Was that a hint? Do you want to get married? We can totally do that here in Connecticut or in New York."

Toby held up his hands. "Whoa! Calm down. We aren't running out to do it right away. We need to do some serious talking about it all, especially if you're going to be climbing mountains, Jensen. I don't know how Cat and Jigger can leave Pamela behind every time."

Jensen lifted one of his shoulders. "To be honest, I think Everest will be Cat's last expedition. She wasn't too upset when our trip got canceled last year, and K2 isn't on her list. She doesn't want to take a chance on leaving Pamela an orphan in case something happens during a climb. She'll do smaller trips in Wyoming and around the country."

"Sounds wise," Toby said, then shivered as a cold breeze blew passed him. "Come on. We either need to finish our run or head home."

"Let's run. We have chocolate cake at home and I want a piece." Jensen added marriage and children to the list of postponed conversations. They would get back to them soon.

Chapter Three

This was one of those uninhibited dreams that come free with growing up. I was sure that mine about Everest was not mine alone; the highest point on earth, unattainable, foreign to all experience, was there for many boys and grown men to aspire toward.

– Thomas F. Hornbein

Toby groaned when they got back to the house. As the sun set, the temperature had dropped and they'd run faster to get back home before it got too cold. He hadn't run that fast in a long time. His legs protested as he dashed up the front steps then jogged in place until Jensen finally got the door open.

"Holy shit!" He chaffed his hands. "It got cold out there."

Jensen nodded. "Yeah. Let's go grab a shower. Just be careful about the water. Don't start it out hot. Do it cool and we'll slowly warm it up."

He wasn't looking forward to that experience. "Why don't we just wait until we're warm before we take a shower? I really don't want to take a cold shower. We can have some cake."

It was a bribe, but Toby didn't care. He didn't like being cold and if getting Jensen to eat dessert with him meant he could take a warm shower, then he'd do it. Shaking his head, Jensen locked the door before taking a hold of Toby's hand and escorting him upstairs.

"I want dessert, but not cake. My dessert's going help me burn some more calories, warm us up and get us even more sweaty." Jensen leered at him.

Toby didn't argue. He'd much rather make love with Jensen then eat any day. He took the hem of Jensen's sweatshirt in his fingers, lifting it up over his head. Jensen raised his arms to help him. They didn't say anything while they finished undressing.

Once they were naked, Toby gripped Jensen's hips, easing his chilled body against Jensen's. He sucked in a deep breath and shivered. Jensen leaned down to nibble along Toby's jaw to his mouth. Moaning softly, Toby opened to Jensen's questing tongue.

While they kissed, Toby slipped his hands around to squeeze Jensen's ass. Then he trailed one set of his fingers along Jensen's crease to tease his hole. Jensen rose up on his feet, but pushed back into his touch.

Toby broke the kiss, dropping his lips to the soft triangle of skin at the base of Jensen's throat. He sucked hard, leaving a mark there, claiming Jensen for all to see. He brought his hand up to Jensen's mouth.

"Get them wet," he ordered. He knew Jensen liked a little bit of burn, so they didn't always use a lot of lube when Toby topped.

While Jensen sucked and licked, Toby leaned farther down to press the tip of his tongue to one of Jensen's nipples. Then he nipped at it, making Jensen jerk slightly. Toby pinched it between his teeth and tugged, playing as much as he could until Jensen tapped the back of his head.

Easing away, he looked at Jensen. "Done?"

Jensen whirled out of his embrace then bent over to brace his elbows on the edge of the mattress. He arched his back, sticking his butt out for Toby.

"I take that as a yes," Toby joked.

He spread Jensen's lightly furred cheeks to expose his puckered opening. Toby ghosted a touch over that hole then pushed one finger in slowly, but not stopping. Jensen tensed for a second before inhaling and relaxing as best as he could. Toby slid it out then pressed two in.

"Oh," Jensen gasped, moving away a little, but Toby kept going.

He knew he wasn't hurting his lover. It was probably a slight burn that would turn into pleasure once Jensen was stretched more. Jensen lifted his left leg onto the bed to give Toby even more access.

Soon he had three fingers buried in Jensen's channel and he was nailing Jensen's gland with every stroke. Jensen panted while rocking back. Toby smiled as Jensen raised up to get hold of his own cock. While Toby kept it up, he watched while Jensen jerked off.

"Toby." Jensen's tone held a touch of pleading.

"Are you ready for me? Do you want me to fuck you, Jensen?" Toby smacked the butt cheek in front of him.

"Yes. Please." Jensen shot him a needy glance over his shoulder.

Toby reached over to the nightstand where he was pretty sure he'd stuffed the slick that morning after he'd made the bed that morning. He made sure to keep stretching Jensen while he got the lube out and popped the top open with his teeth. After squirting some on his cock, he got the bottle closed before dropping it on the floor next to his feet.

He coated his length then positioned it at Jensen's opening. His lover moaned as Toby eased his fingers out before he pressed in to replace them. Once his groin brushed against Jensen's ass, he paused enough to let him adjust to being that full.

Jensen shoved back toward him, giving him the signal to move. He whimpered as Toby grabbed his hips to slip out then slam back in. As they rocked together, their harsh breaths filled the air and Toby did his best to drive Jensen over the edge.

"More, Toby. Please God, harder." Jensen undulated, fucking his own hand while Toby took him.

Toby did as Jensen demanded, his own rhythm losing its fluidity. Pressure built behind his balls. It wasn't until Jensen came, clenching around Toby's cock like a vise, that his own climax hit him hard and he filled Jensen with his hot cum.

Jensen spilled his own over his hand and their comforter. They collapsed into a trembling heap on the floor as Toby softened and slid from Jensen, who lay panting in his arms. Stroking his hand over his lover's shoulders and back, Toby waited until his heart stopped pounding before he pushed to his feet.

He helped Jensen up. They stumbled into the bathroom where Toby propped Jensen against the wall while he got the shower going. Once it was warm enough, he maneuvered them into the large space. Grunting, Jensen braced his hands on the tile and Toby grabbed the soap from the ledge.

After building up some lather, he washed Jensen's body, taking care to clean off all trace of his cum. He washed and rinsed his short hair then traced his fingers over the many scars covering his lover's skin from Jensen's many climbing trips.

When he finished, Jensen returned the favor, though Toby didn't have any scars because he'd never climbed a mountain or risked his life in any way. Yet there were times when he thought the scars on his heart should show on his skin, but he always had a feeling that each time Jensen returned, his broken heart healed a little more.

They wandered out to the bedroom where they stood staring at the messed up comforter. Jensen laughed and said, "I'll take it downstairs and throw it in the washer. Since it was my cum that got all over the thing."

"I'll grab another comforter from the closet. Why don't you bring up a piece of cake and some glasses of milk? We'll have a snack before bed." Toby placed a kiss on Jensen's shoulder before heading to the guest bedroom where they kept their extra blankets.

By the time Toby wrestled one of them out of the bag, Jensen had stuffed them in and got back to the other room, Jensen was sitting in the middle of the mattress, naked and sucking a gob of chocolate frosting off his finger. Toby bit his lip to stop from uttering the groan threatening to escape him. He wanted Jensen's lips wrapped around his cock and that tongue licking his length.

"Come on." Jensen patted the bed next to him. "This is some good cake, even if I say so myself."

Toby set the blanket at the foot of the bed then climbed in beside Jensen, settling before sticking his finger in the frosting. He held it up to Jensen's lips and his lover smiled as he stuck out his tongue to swipe it through the chocolate.

"Christ! I want your mouth on my cock," Toby whimpered.

"Your wish is my command."

Jensen pushed him so he lay back, head on the pillow while Jensen wiggled his way between Toby's thighs. Then he smeared chocolate frosting all over Toby's erection. Toby couldn't help but laugh as he looked down to see Jensen eyeing his length as though it was the best dessert he'd ever seen.

"I can't wait to feel you clean this mess off me, but I'm not sure I can watch you do it," Toby admitted, so he let his head drop back and he closed his eyes.

Another whimper emerged when warmth and suction surrounded his cock. He reached down to thread his fingers through Jensen's hair, holding him there with his nose pressed into Toby's pubic hair for a second before letting up on the pressure. Jensen popped up to glare at him and Toby grinned.

"Prick," Jensen muttered, but he ducked back down to begin feasting on the icing still covering Toby.

"Oh shit," Toby murmured, smoothing his hand over Jensen's head then running his fingers down to the hollow of Jensen's cheek from the suction he placed around Toby's shaft.

Slow and easy while he thrust up into Jensen's mouth, doing his best not to go too deep because he didn't want to choke him. Jensen let him do as he wanted while he cleaned him off. Toby shuddered when Jensen reached between his legs to take his balls and tug on them lightly.

"Jensen, I'm close," he warned as his orgasm built. It wasn't going to be as intense as his first one earlier, but it would still rock his world. Toby knew that.

Jensen pressed just the tip of his finger against Toby's hole then as he took Toby all the way down, he shoved it in, causing Toby to come with a cry.

"Fuck!"

He curled up over Jensen's head, holding his shoulders while he emptied his balls. Jensen drank as much of it as he could, but some trickled out of the corner of his mouth. When Toby was finished, Jensen surged up to take Toby's lips.

As they kissed, Toby wrapped his hand around Jensen's cock, knowing he was close as well. The taste of himself on Jensen's tongue made Toby give another spurt of cum which he scooped up to create a small slick layer to ease the friction of his hand on Jensen.

Jensen broke their kiss, throwing his head back as he came all over Toby's hand and stomach. He kept pumping until Jensen grimaced because his shaft was sensitive. Toby gave him a peck, licking some of his own cum off Jensen's chin before he rolled out of the bed.

After picking up the plate and setting it on the dresser, he strolled to the bathroom to get a cloth. He washed himself then took it back to Jensen and cleaned him up. Toby tossed it toward the hamper before climbing under the blankets.

He encircled Jensen's waist, pulling him back against his chest. He sighed as they wiggled to find the perfect spot for both of them. Once he was satisfied, Toby exhaled slowly.

Jensen covered his hand with his. "When I was in rehab, I used to dream of us sleeping like this."

"Really? What else did you dream about while you were getting better?"

They hadn't really discussed what had gone on during rehab for Jensen. While Toby had been falling apart because the man he loved had disappeared, Jensen had been in a true fight for the rest of his life. If he hadn't gotten control of his addiction, Jensen would've died eventually, and Toby would've lost Jensen forever, not just for six years.

Hell, even him going away for months at a time to climb mountains wasn't as hard as him falling off the face of the earth without so much as a phone call. At least with the trips, Toby knew where he was, even if he couldn't talk to him sometimes.

"I dreamed of standing on top of a mountain. It was like I was the only person left on earth," Jensen said softly.

Toby wasn't surprised by that dream. It had to be lonely while at the center. Sure, there had been people there to help Jensen, like counselors and doctors. Hell, even the other patients could've been seen as support in a way since they knew what Jensen was going through. Yet there wasn't one person there who had known him from his previous life. No one he could've counted as a friend.

At least that was the feeling Toby had gotten from what little Jensen had told him. Jensen had emerged from the program strong and clean, with a new passion for climbing the world's highest mountains and two new friends. While he'd had one relapse, he hadn't gotten lost in the drugs and alcohol again.

He'd returned to Toby a changed man. A better man as well, and Toby found himself falling deeper in love with Jensen every day.

"Is that dream why you want to summit Everest? To stand at the top of the world and see how small you are in the grand scheme of things?" Toby got where a mountain could make a man feel like that.

Jensen shrugged. "I don't need to be reminded how insignificant I am in the world, Toby. I learned that lesson early on in life."

Toby shifted and wiggled them until Jensen lay on his back and Toby propped himself up over him to look down.

"Don't you dare say you're not important or you're insignificant, Jensen. You're the most important thing in my world and when you're not here, I miss you. It's like there's a giant hole in my life that nothing except you will fill." He glared at Jensen.

Smiling, Jensen cradled Toby's face in his hands. "I know that. Why do you think I came back to you? You were the only person I wanted to see as soon as I got out of rehab. In my dream, I'd stand on the top of the mountain, feeling like I was the only person in the world then it was like your voice would invade my mind and all I knew was there was someone out there who had cared about me at some point. I would pray that you would give me another chance, once I got my act together."

"Why didn't you return right after you got out?" Toby nuzzled Jensen's palm.

"I might have been clean, but I certainly didn't have myself together. I had to figure out a way to function without the numbness — a way to accept all the shit I couldn't do anything about while fixing what I could. I didn't want you to become my next addiction, Toby. I didn't want to force you to be the 'sane' one while I worked the rest of my shit out."

"I would've done it. I would've gladly been the one you leaned on while you got better," he whispered.

Jensen curled up to press a kiss on his lips. "I know that, but I didn't want that for you. It's not healthy. I needed to find my own strength, so I could lean on myself first. Trust me, even sober, it wasn't pretty there for a year or two after rehab. There were times when Jigger and Cat didn't even want to be around me."

Toby frowned and Jensen grimaced, obviously trying to think of a better way to explain what he meant.

"Leaning is a two-way street. If I'm to lean on you, you have to have the trust that I'll be here for you to lean on as well. Do you understand that?"

He nodded.

"But for a while there, I wasn't strong enough to be leaned against. I wouldn't have been able to be the foundation you needed to build any dream on. I wasn't stable and my own core was built on shifting sand for a long time." Jensen closed his eyes and took a deep breath. "As I learned how to climb, I learned to be patient and to become a person others could trust to be there to help them find their way up or down the mountain. Eventually I discovered I trusted myself not to crumble if things got tough. I wouldn't reach for drugs—or alcohol—to get me through the trouble. I need a clear mind when I climb. A mistake of a millimeter could be life—or death—and I won't risk that for myself, you or any of my climbing partners."

"Thank you for including me in that," Toby told him.

"Of course. You're foremost in my mind when I'm climbing."

"God, I hope not." Toby tried to sound horrified. "You need to keep your brain a hundred percent focused on the trail ahead of you."

Jensen punched him in the chest and they laughed while Toby rubbed the spot.

"You know what I'm talking about. You're the reason I take every precaution to get up and down the mountains safely. I know you're waiting for me and I refuse not to come back to you. I did that once and it hurt both of us."

It had hurt them both. Toby knew that and it was one of the reasons why he still had doubts buried deep in his soul about Jensen sticking around. Yet it was something he had to work through on his own because Jensen was doing as he promised and kept returning.

"I appreciate the caution." Toby rested his fingertips on Jensen's chest over his heart. "I'm getting used to having you around. I'd hate to have to learn how to live without you again."

A yawn surprised him and Jensen chuckled.

"We need to get some sleep. You have work in the morning and I have to start getting my shit organized for the trip."

There was some bumping and shoving as they got situated on the bed again, blankets covering them. Toby kissed Jensen goodnight.

"Dream about something amazing tonight," he ordered.

"I'll dream about you," Jensen replied.

Chapter Four

At the end of the valley and above the glacier Everest rises,
not so much a peak as a prodigious mountain-mass…the
highest of the world's mountains, it seems, has to make but
a single gesture of magnificence to be lord of all, vast in
unchallenged and isolated supremacy.

— George Mallory

"I ordered a new sleeping bag," Jensen told Jigger as
he propped his phone between his shoulder and his
ear, so he could type in his address on the website.

"Good. The one you've been using is a wreck, dude,
and there's no way it'll keep you warm enough in Base
Camp." Jigger snorted. "I just emailed the company
we're going through. Looks like there'll be about eight
of us on this expedition, along with three guides. I'm
not sure how many Sherpas they'll be using. Their
contact guy is emailing me a list of shit they suggest we
take with us."

"Are we going to be able to do this, Jigger?" Jensen
hit the Buy button then stood to wander to the French

doors leading into the backyard. He stared out over the white blanket of snow that had fallen overnight.

The storm had started yesterday afternoon and had been so bad, Toby had chosen to stay in the city at Simpson's apartment rather than driving in it. Jensen had agreed with him, not wanting Toby to risk his life trying to get back to home, though he hated how quiet the house was without Toby around to yell at him about the laundry or why the bed wasn't made yet. He could just imagine the fit Toby would have when he saw the mess Jensen had made in one of the spare rooms.

He'd pulled out all of his climbing gear to go over and see what he needed to replace. He wasn't going to go to Everest with old rope or anything that might give out on him while climbing the Khumbu Icefall or along the Hillary Step. Both were dangerous, even with brand new equipment. All of his stuff was strewn across the floor and every available piece of furniture.

"We can do this, Jensen. This has been one of our goals since we placed our feet at the base of our first mountain and chose to go up instead of down. It won't be easy, but we knew that." Jigger cleared his throat. "We're going with one of the most reputable Everest climbing companies, and we have some experience at high altitudes, plus the three of us have climbed together before. We trust each other. If there's going to be any trouble, I want to be in it with you and Cat. The two of you will get my ass down off that mountain."

He braced his hand on the door then rested his forehead on his biceps. Closing his eyes, he remembered the expression on Toby's face when he told him about going to Everest. "Toby's scared to death about this trip. Even more, I think, than any of the others I've gone on since we got back together."

"Of course he's scared."

Jensen jerked when Cat's voice came over the phone. Either he was on speaker and didn't know it or she'd taken the phone from Jigger and heard what he'd said.

"Your Toby is an intelligent man. He might not be a climber, but he knows that Everest isn't a cakewalk. I'm sure he's probably done research on the mountain, especially now that he knows we're going there."

"He needs to know all the information he can on things. Makes him a great investment planner since he'll dig through all mentions of a stock to make sure it's the right one for his clients. But it isn't the greatest trait when it's something like Everest. He's going to focus on the accidents and deaths." He thumped his head against his arm. "He'll hug me and whisper 'I love you' when I leave, while he's dying inside, worried I won't come back this time."

Cat sighed. "He knows you'll come back. You haven't broken that promise yet."

Jensen snorted. "There's always a first time for everything, Cat, and the wounds from me leaving all those years ago haven't completely healed yet. He knows the odds are against us."

"You do know that at some time we all reach a point that what—or who—we leave behind becomes more important than what we're heading toward. If you've reached that point, Jensen, we won't think any worse about you than we already do." Cat laughed.

"Bitch. It's not that. I just don't want him to worry while I'm gone. I hate thinking of him pacing the floors, imagining all the worse scenarios of what can happen on the trip."

Turning his back on the snow, he wandered back to his desk and his laptop. He saw that his transaction had gone through, so he sat to see about ordering some new

Gore-Tex jackets for layering while on the mountain. He'd already purchased a couple of fleeces, plus a new, light down jacket.

"You know that this will be my last high altitude climb, right?"

She was quiet for a minute and Jensen tried to figure out if she wanted him to answer or if it was rhetorical. Before he could speak up, Cat spoke again.

"Now that we have Pamela, I can't take the risk of something happening during a climb. I don't want her to lose both of her parents because we're addicted to the thrill of cheating death. Once I summit Everest and descend safely, I'll be happy with the climbs here in the states. There are a few that can get my heart racing enough."

"If you feel that way, why even go with us? Why not just stay here if your heart isn't in it anymore?" He understood where Cat was coming from though.

"Because I want to show my father that I'm capable of doing something he never could. He tried to summit Everest two different climbs and turned back each time. The bastard needs to see that I'm not useless or weak, just because I'm a girl." She growled.

"No bitterness there at all," he teased, though he knew all about Cat's father's disdain for his daughter and didn't blame her at all for wanting to rub his nose in it.

There sounded like wrestling on the other end of the line and he wondered what the hell was going on. Next thing, he heard Jigger.

"Great, man. Now I'm going to have to listen to her rant about that asshole. Thanks a lot," Jigger complained.

"Hey, that wasn't my fault. She went there." He pulled up the website for Gore-Tex. "I know better than to talk about her father with her."

Jigger grumbled something that he couldn't make out, and he wasn't interested in finding out what Jigger had said. There was no love lost between Jigger and his father-in-law either.

"Have you heard from Ransom yet about the K2 permit?" He probably shouldn't be looking ahead to a possible assault on K2, yet if he had an idea that it was going to happen, he would have a chance to prepare Toby for that eventual reality.

"Totally forgot to tell you. Yeah, he called about two days ago. We're going to Pakistan next year and taking the Abruzzi Spur. It's what the government's letting us climb, so while we won't be trying any of the harder routes, we'll still get to conquer the Savage Mountain." Jigger sounded excited.

"Great." He wished he could sound just as thrilled, but his stomach dropped when he heard they had permission.

"I don't think you're as happy as I thought you would be when I heard the news. We'll have climbed the two highest mountains in the world within a year of each other. I never thought I'd get to Everest, much less K2."

Jensen could almost see Jigger bouncing around the living room in Wyoming, pumping his fists. Out of the three of them, Jigger was the most fanatical about mountaineering. After getting clean from his own narcotic habit, Jigger had discovered the natural high one could get from conquering a mountain. He'd introduced Cat to the joys of high altitude climbing. She wanted to prove her father wrong about women, so she took to the danger and excitement of risking her life on the rocks of the mountains.

Jensen had started doing it to keep from thinking about shooting up or snorting whatever he could find to numb the pain. Then he'd discovered he liked it—or he had until he'd reconnected with Toby. Now leaving for months at time was wearing thin and the expeditions were losing the sparkle they once had.

"Well, your dream will be coming true soon enough. Now go calm your wife down before she frightens Pamela," Jensen told his friend. "Don't forget to email me the list the company sends you. I want to make sure I have everything on it before I ship my shit out to your place. Tell Cat I love her and give your daughter a hug for me."

"All right, Jensen. I'll call you on Friday and we'll start figuring out logistics of getting all of our stuff to Nepal." Jigger hung up.

Jensen tossed his phone on the desk, not even caring when it slid across the surface then landed on the floor. Leaning back in his chair, he glanced around the room and his gaze skipped lightly over all the framed photos on the walls and the bookshelves. He knew they were from different climbs he'd done over the years. There was a large empty space above the fireplace mantel. He'd reserved that for summit pictures of him at Everest and K2.

He'd always vowed that once he'd done those two mountains, he'd cut back on his climbing. Hell, he didn't have to leave the States if he was looking for technically difficult climbs. There were some places in the Rockies or out in the Cascades where he could get his thrills without spending half the year away. If he wanted dangerous, he could climb Mount Washington in New Hampshire. The weather there alone could kill a person. Maybe he could even convince Toby to go with him.

After pushing to his feet, he stalked over to one picture that was set on a high shelf where he didn't have to see it every time he walked in, not if he didn't want to. Jensen pulled it down then studied the people in the photo. No one had been happy about being together and having their portrait done. Yet it had been something his mother wanted, so they'd done it. His father had been an absolute drunken bastard most of Jensen's life, but there were moments when he'd tried to make Jensen's mom happy. It was weird to have a moment where they were all smiling captured forever on a piece of film.

"Are those your parents?"

Jensen jumped and fumbled with the frame, barely catching it before it hit the floor. As much as he hated it, he didn't want it ruined. He set it back on the shelf then turned to see Toby in the doorway of the study, hip propped against the wall and arms folded over his chest.

"I didn't hear you get home," Jensen said, smiling and hoping Toby wouldn't press him about the past. He'd had to talk about it during rehab and that had been more than enough discussion for the rest of his life.

"You were talking to Jigger and Cat. I didn't want to interrupt. How are they doing?"

He watched as Toby pushed away from where he stood and strolled across the room to him. Toby reached out, making Jensen's smile disappear when he picked up the photo.

"They're doing good. Cat sends her love. She hopes you can come out for a little vacation when I go out there to do some conditioning next month." He tried to grab the frame from Toby, but his lover kept moving it away.

Toby nodded. "I think I can get some time off. Just let me know when and I'll put in a request for it. Maybe you can teach me how to downhill ski."

Jensen grinned. "That would be awesome. I bet you would like that and Pamela will love getting to see her uncle Toby."

"She's a good kid." Toby waved the frame in front of him. "Now are you going to answer my question? Is this your family? I got to thinking about it earlier today when Simpson said something about going to visit his parents this weekend that we never really talked about your parents. Every time I bring them up, you change the subject."

"There's nothing to talk about. We were just an average family except I drank from a young age." He finally managed to snatch it from Toby's hand then set it on the shelf before he stalked away. Stuffing his hands in his pockets, he glared at the floor where he stood in the middle of the room.

Toby took his hand, tugging him toward the couch where he shoved Jensen down onto the cushions. "No running away from this, Jensen. It's time we talked about something from your past. It's like you've chosen to remember only back to a certain point. Anything that happened before that no longer exists."

He stiffened, not wanting to tell Toby how depressing his family had really been. He'd met Toby's parents and sisters during Christmas last year when they'd come to stay with them for the holiday. Toby's dad was an electrician who was as blue collar as they came, yet he'd enjoyed all the little gadgets Toby had given him as gifts. It was obvious Mr. Schwartzel was proud of his son, even though he wasn't entirely sure about the gay thing. He never treated Jensen with anything other than respect.

Toby's mother was tiny and plump. She'd slowed down a lot over the last year because of a bad hip, but she didn't let that stop her from ice skating or going out and building snowmen with her children and grandchildren. After they'd arrived, she'd taken over the kitchen to cook Christmas dinner and refused all offers of help.

Jensen had seen families like the Schwartzels back in his hometown. He'd just figured it was all a show. That once they got behind the doors of their homes, the truth came out—like at his house with his father.

"My father wasn't like yours," he blurted, then wanted to bite his tongue.

Chapter Five

If you always put limits on everything you do, physical or anything else. It will spread into your work and into your life. There are no limits. There are only plateaus, and you must not stay there, you must go beyond them.

– Bruce Lee

"No. He didn't look like a poor kid from Philly," Toby commented as he joined Jensen on the couch, placing his hand on Jensen's knee, which was bouncing in a clear sign of his agitation.

"Not what I meant, though that's true. Dad came from new money. My great-grandfather got in on the ground level when the automobiles started becoming big. By the time my dad came around, the family owned several car dealerships and garages. My mom came from old money—like came across on the Mayflower old." Jensen really looked reluctant to talk about his family and Toby wanted to know why.

He had a feeling it really was the foundation of why Jensen started drinking when he was so young, and why the ambition to make money had driven him to such lengths.

"I told you when I showed back up that my family was awesome and it was me that was a fuck-up," Jensen reminded Toby.

Nodding, Toby said, "Right. You mentioned something about you being the one who didn't know how to love—or something like that."

Jensen jumped to his feet then started pacing in front of him. "Right. I still think that's true."

"Bullshit." Toby grinned when Jensen paused to stare at him. "You've told me so many time how much you love me. I'm pretty sure there's nothing wrong with your emotions. I think your problem was figuring out how to deal with them."

Dismissing Toby's words with a flap of his hand, Jensen shook his head. "Whatever. The thing is my family wasn't the perfect one that everyone thought we were. My parents were really good at appearing to be what others thought they should be."

He curled up in the corner of the couch, tucking his legs under his ass while he watched Jensen walk restlessly around the room. "You don't look too unhappy in that photo."

"It's the only one I kept when I left to go to school. As much as I knew it was a lie, I liked that I could point to it and tell everyone how great my family was." He shoved his hand through his hair and Toby wished he could do something to ease his pain a little. "My dad was an alcoholic and my mom abused prescription drugs before it was fashionable to do so."

"I'm sorry. Was your dad abusive to you or your mom?" He didn't like the idea of Jensen being hurt by anyone.

Jensen shook his head. "No. I know a lot of people would just assume he would be, but it wasn't like that. They argued all the time. She wanted to travel around the world like she used to before she got married and my dad drank to try and drown out her bitching. Neither of them was abusive to me. They simply ignored me until I turned sixteen, when they shipped me off to boarding school. That way, my dad could bury his head in his work and my mother could fly around the world with her friends."

Toby frowned. "You drank because you were lonely?"

"It numbed the pain of knowing my parents didn't want me around. At first I did it to be cool while hanging out with the other kids. Then it got to the point where I couldn't get moving in the morning without having a drink. It snowballed from there until I was drinking most of the day. I'd learned how to disguise it." Jensen shrugged. "I was good at that."

He could admit that was true. He'd never known just how much Jensen drank while they were dating. Toby had always thought it was social drinking like he'd done while at clubs and parties. Little had he known Jensen had kept a bottle in his desk to get him through the day.

"You learned your destructive behavior from your parents, where most kids learn shit like that," Toby muttered. "Are they still alive?"

"Yeah. I haven't seen them since I graduated from boarding school. They didn't come to my college graduation and I haven't talked them in years. Not sure where either of them are, though I know Dad sold off the dealerships and the garages when he realized I wasn't interested in running them." Jensen went over to the doors and pressed his hands against the windows. "God knows where my mom is."

Toby pursed his lips, trying to figure out what to say or how to approach the subject. "Do you think that seeing them might help?"

Swinging around to look at him, Jensen asked, "Help with what?"

"I don't know. Your recovery, I guess. I mean you've been sober for five years and off the drugs for two years now. Isn't it time to face them and see them as the fallible creatures they are instead of the indifferent monsters you remember them as?" Toby plucked at a frayed rip in his jeans. "At least find out where they are and go to show them what you've become without any help from them."

"What? Rub their faces in the fact that I'm a recovering alcoholic and a former drug user? I've turned out just like them." Jensen turned away from him. "I'm not sure that's a shining example of being a success."

"Yes you're those things, but you're also an accomplished mountaineer who has climbed some of the most dangerous and highest mountains in the world. Not everyone can say they've done that and you've done it after cleaning up your act." Toby let his gaze trail over Jensen from the back of his head over his firm ass to his bare feet. "You're a man any father would be proud of. Hell, my dad brags about you to all of his friends every time you summit a mountain."

Jensen chuckled. "He does?"

Toby laughed as well. "Oh yeah. Seems like climbing mountains and battling nature makes better bragging material than what I do."

He shifted on the couch when Jensen came to kneel next to him. Jensen took his hand in his hand and squeezed it.

"Your dad loves and respects you very much, Toby. I hear it in his voice and see it on his face every time he looks at you." Jensen was rather earnest.

"I know that, love. Don't worry about me. I'm not jealous. I just wanted to let you know how much my dad respects you too. He considers you another son." Toby laughed. "In fact, you're more the son he wished I'd been."

That knowledge didn't bother Toby either. He'd known that he wasn't exactly the son his dad had hoped he'd be when he was born. His dad had wanted a son who liked sports and cars. While Toby liked to watch sporting events, he wasn't interested in playing in any of them. He knew nothing more than the usual about cars.

Growing up, he'd liked numbers and found out he was good with them. Dad accepted that and never made Toby feel like he was a disappointment. Yet he'd seen how happy Dad was when he met Jensen and realized that Toby's boyfriend was athletic and loved cars, which Toby hadn't known about Jensen.

"Don't say that. Your dad loves you." Jensen frowned, looking worried that Toby might really think his dad loved Jensen more.

Toby erased the creases on Jensen's forehead with his fingers. "Don't worry, Jensen. I know Dad loves me. I'm not jealous of your relationship with him. I'm really thrilled that my family has taken to you as well as they have. I'll be honest. They've never loved any of my former boyfriends that they'd met, not that I took many of them home."

"It wasn't until I met you that I thought about what being part of a couple involved and I managed to screw that up." Jensen took Toby's fingers then pressed them to his lips.

"You fixed it when you came back," he said quickly, not wanting to listen to Jensen beat himself up again for leaving. "When you get back from Everest, we'll head up to my parents' for a couple days, so my mom can spoil you and you can tell my dad all about your trip. He'll love to see the pictures and stuff."

Before Jensen could say anything else, Toby leaned forward to replace his fingers with his lips on Jensen's mouth. He hummed softly when Jensen opened for him and he swept his tongue in. He slid his hand around the back of Jensen's head to grip his neck, holding him still while he took control of the kiss.

Jensen relaxed into his touch, allowing Toby to do what he wanted. What Toby wanted was Jensen's cock inside him right then. After shoving at Jensen's shoulders so he flopped back on the couch, Toby straddled his thighs then rocked his jean-covered hard-on into Jensen's.

"Is there something you want?" Jensen smirked and Toby slid one of his hands up under Jensen's shirt to pinch his nipple. "Holy fuck!"

Arching his back, Jensen hissed a little. It didn't take long for Toby to have both of their shirts off and his fingers on those two pieces of flesh. He tugged, twisted and flicked them until Jensen whined and they were red from the abuse. Leaning down, Toby licked one then blew a puff of air over it.

"Oh God," Jensen moaned, cupping Toby's head and not allowing him to move away.

"You need to let me go," Toby mumbled. "I want us naked and you inside me."

"Do you want to go upstairs?" Jensen put his hands on either side of his hips as though he was going to help Toby stand.

Shaking his head, Toby grinned. "I want you to fuck me right here."

Jensen's eyes went wide at Toby's blunt statement, which made Toby burst out laughing. It wasn't as if he hadn't demanded to be fucked before, but it seemed like Jensen was always shocked when he did it.

After climbing off, Toby stripped quickly before kneeling in front of Jensen. He didn't fumble or anything as he unbuckled Jensen's belt then unbuttoned and unzipped his jeans. Tapping at Jensen's waist, he nodded when he lifted his hips so Toby could yank his pants down.

"Going commando today," he said in approval. "Less clothes I need to deal with."

Once he'd exposed Jensen's cock, Toby dropped his head to wrap his lips around the thick girth. Jensen was about the same length as Toby, but he was thicker. The thought made Toby's ass clench. God, he couldn't wait to get it inside him.

He took Jensen all the way down then swallowed around him. Jensen jerked and moaned. Toby worked the shaft in his mouth, sucking until he could lick drops of pre-cum from Jensen's slit.

Jensen smoothed his hand over Toby's head. "God, I love your mouth almost as much as I love your ass. We don't have any lube down here though. I don't want to hurt you."

Toby didn't really listen as he moved his mouth from Jensen's length to his balls. He sucked them in one at a time, playing with them while Jensen babbled. It wasn't until Jensen tugged on his hair that Toby refocused on Jensen's face.

"What?" he asked after rising up on his knees away from Jensen.

"Lube. We need some because I don't want to fuck you without it." Jensen looked like he was going to get up and leave.

Pinning his hips to the couch, Toby shook his head. "Don't worry about it. We'll take it slow. I don't want to waste any more time. I want you to fuck me, Jensen. The pain isn't important."

And it wasn't. He knew it would hurt a little when they began, but eventually it would morph into pleasure and that was what he yearned for. He straddled Jensen's hips again before pressing his fingers against Jensen's lips. His lover opened and sucked them in, getting them as wet as he could.

When Toby thought it was enough, he reached around and shoved his fingers into his ass. "Argh!" He grunted.

Jensen grabbed his hips. "Don't. I'm going to get the lube."

Toby put his other hand on Jensen's chest, stopping him from moving. "No. I'll be all right."

He rushed through stretching his opening and once he thought it was good enough, he removed his fingers. Jensen grabbed his cock then held it still while Toby positioned himself over it. Toby bit his bottom lip as he lowered his body to take Jensen in. As much as he wanted to rush, he eased down inch by inch, waiting for a second as he adjusted to being invaded.

Once he bottomed out, he rested his hands on Jensen's chest for support while he panted. Jensen didn't move either as he kept his gaze on Toby. Finally, Toby relaxed and groaned.

He pushed up on his knees then dropped. Jensen gripped Toby's waist, surging up to meet each downward movement. When the flared head of Jensen's cock nailed his gland, Toby shouted, "Fuck!"

Trembling, he began to move faster, needing more. Suddenly, Jensen wrapped him in a tight embrace, and somehow without sliding out of him, got them on the floor with Jensen on top. Toby's ankles rested on his lover's shoulders and he was almost bent in half as Jensen slammed into him hard.

"Yes," Toby encouraged him. "More. I'm so close."

Jensen grunted, seemingly caught up in fucking him as he wanted. There would be bruises on his skin from where Jensen gripped him and Toby knew he'd be feeling Jensen for the next couple of days.

His climax raced through him without a touch to his cock. He spilled cum over his stomach and clenched tight around Jensen, whose rhythm stuttered for a second then he slammed deep inside. Jensen cried out as he flooded Toby's ass before collapsing on top of him.

Toby grimaced at the rather chilly mess between them, yet he loved the feeling of Jensen's cum inside him. "I'll never get used to that feeling," he muttered, tracing circles on Jensen's shoulder blades.

"I know," Jensen agreed.

They were lying there, basking the aftermath of their mutual climaxes when the doorbell rang. Jensen jerked away from him, and Toby winced as he slid out of him.

"Are you expecting someone?"

"Aww...shit! Yeah, Simpson said he wanted to go over some files with me and I told him to come out for dinner. He's going to spend the night and head back to the city in the morning with me." Toby glanced down at his cum-covered body and laughed. "I'm pretty sure he doesn't want to see me like this."

Jensen snatched up one of their shirts before wiping himself off. He did up his jeans then held out a hand. "Run up the back stairs to the bedroom. Take a quick shower and change. I can entertain him until you get back down here."

Toby let Jensen help him up. He kissed him before he gathered up his clothes and dashed through the hallway to the kitchen and the stairs. It was great of Jensen to offer to deal with Simpson until Toby cleaned up since they really didn't like each other that much. Oh, they tolerated being around each other for Toby's sake, so at least they acted like adults most of the time.

He grinned as he headed into the bathroom, feeling like a kid who'd been caught with his boyfriend by his parents.

Chapter Six

Cherish your human connections; your relationships with friends and family.

— Joseph Brodsky

Jensen strolled off the plane, keeping a hold of his carry-on along with Toby's hand. He didn't want to get separated from him. Not that the airport was that busy, but still he liked knowing Toby was close by him.

"Jigger going to pick us up?" Toby asked for the six hundredth time.

Okay, so he was exaggerating about how many times Toby had asked, but it had been a couple of times since they'd got on the plane in Connecticut. Toby didn't like flying and one way he coped was to go over their plans obsessively. Jensen dealt with it because he loved Toby and he also knew what it was like to be scared of something.

He hadn't handled his fears quite as well as Toby did. Where Toby tended to ask a ton of questions and talk incessantly, Jensen would've just drunk himself unconscious or shot something up to get through the flight. Of course, flying didn't freak him out, which was a good thing since he had to be on airplanes a lot for his expeditions. Now that they were on the ground, Toby would be fine.

"Yes. He and Pamela will meet us at baggage claim then we'll head out to grab Cat from work. We'll probably get something to eat on the way to their place. I'm not sure how much Cat will want to cook tonight." He'd been through the Laramie airport a hundred times and knew exactly where they had to go.

Toby had been out to visit Cat and Jigger with him before and they got along far better than Jensen and Simpson did. Of course, Simpson was a self-righteous prick who believed that Jensen was going to bail on Toby at some point, no matter how long Jensen had stuck around for.

He ignored the looks they got for holding hands. Jensen didn't care if some people were uncomfortable with two men being together. He wasn't about to make out with Toby in a crowd, but he wouldn't have done that even if they were some place a little more accepting. Jensen didn't really believe in effusive public displays of affection anyway.

"Hey there, man," Jigger called out to him as they approached the baggage claim area.

"Toby. Toby," Pamela chanted from where she stood beside her father.

Toby crouched and held open his arms so Pamela could stagger over to him for a hug. He swept her up before bussing her cheek. She shrieked with laughter and patted his face. Jensen clasped Jigger's hand then slapped his back in the man clasp they'd perfected. Then he tickled Pamela's side and she threw herself at him.

"Whoa there, Pammy." He caught her then she wrapped her arms around his neck and hugged him tight. Jigger and Toby embraced as well. Then the bell went off to warn them their luggage was coming.

"We'll stop and pick up Cat then get some supper on the way to the house," Jigger informed them, just like Jensen had explained to Toby.

While they waited, Pamela demanded to return to Toby and she chattered at him the entire time. Jensen didn't have any real idea of what she was saying, but just having Toby grunt and acknowledge her seemed to be enough to make her happy.

"All your stuff arrived just fine. I have it piled in your old trailer. Cat got it cleaned out for you. Might as well use it while you're here instead of trying to squeeze in with us." Jigger poked Pamela in the side.

She laughed. "Jens sleep wit me."

"Thanks, honey, but I won't fit in your bed," Jensen told her. "Plus where would we put Toby?"

She wrinkled her little nose as she pondered the problem. "Right. Too big. No room."

Jigger and Jensen grabbed the two bags they'd checked while Toby kept Pamela busy. Jensen's friend led the way out of the terminal to the parking lot. Once they were all settled in the SUV, Jensen glanced at Jigger.

"Are we going for a hike tomorrow?"

"You know it, man. Might as well get you started, plus you'll need to start running more. As the weeks go on, we'll start doing some higher treks. My mom's coming in to watch Pamela while we head up into the Rockies for some fourteen thousand foot climbs. By the time we head out to Nepal, we'll be as ready as we can be." Jigger sniggered.

"No one is ready for Everest," Jensen muttered. "Not even guys who guide it are ready. Every minute on the mountain is different than it was the year before."

Jigger nodded. "People think mountains are these giant immovable objects, but the rocks tumbles and the glaciers melt. Snow falls and ice breaks. At the summit, you look down and all you see are the same clouds you saw while you were climbing up."

Toby made a sound and Jensen glanced at him. He saw Toby swallow before flashing him a trembling smile. Twisting in his seat, Jensen stretched out to touch Toby. He tried to make his own smile reassuring, but he knew it wasn't a good effort.

The silence alerted Jigger something was up and he met Jensen's gaze for a second before using the rear view mirror to catch Toby's eyes. "I'm not going to insult you by telling you not to worry. You wouldn't be human — or in love with this guy here — if you didn't get freaked out about him going to Everest. Any kind of climbing is dangerous and anyone doing it should approach it with caution."

"We've been doing this together for a few years now, Toby. There's only one person I'd trust more to watch my back and that would be you." He squeezed Toby's knee before settling back in his seat. "Have you talked to Cat about teaching Toby her world famous fried chicken recipe?"

They all knew he was changing the subject and Jigger let it happen.

"You're going to have to bribe her. She's never even showed me how to make it." Jigger shook his head.

"Don't worry. I know just what I can give her to get that recipe from her." Toby wiggled his eyebrows at Pamela and the little girl squealed with joy.

"What?" Both Jensen and Jigger asked.

Toby shrugged. "I'm not telling you. One of the things I'm going to do is promise not to share it with the two of you. If she wanted you to have it, she would've given it to you a while ago."

"He has a point," Jensen told his friend.

Jigger sighed. "I know. Okay, here's Cat's place. I'll run in and get her."

Once Jigger strolled toward the building, Jensen turned to look at Toby. "I'm sorry about that."

"About what? What Jigger said about mountains?" At Jensen's nod, Toby flapped his hand in dismissal. "Don't be. I'm not an idiot. I realize all of that stuff, but I have to say everything is dangerous. Hell, I hate flying because all I can think about is all the things that can go wrong while we're up in the air. Nothing's safe, no matter how much we'd like to believe it to be so."

"Right, but I don't want you to dwell on it while you're here. You're going back home in four days then I won't see you for five months. I'd like this time to be happy memories for the times when you get freaked out—or worried. You can look back on them and smile."

Toby unhooked his seat belt then edged closer to Jensen. He leaned forward to kiss him, quick and gentle. With Pamela in the car as well, they couldn't get too hot or heavy.

"Any time I get to spend with you—whether here or at home—is happy for me. I'm not going to tell you I won't worry and that there are going to be days where I hate you because you're gone. You're too smart not to realize I'm going to feel those emotions while you're away. But I can promise that I will welcome you home with a hug and a kiss, plus some other things that we can't discuss in front of a certain little girl." Toby winked before easing back to buckle back up.

Before Jensen could reply, his door popped open and he struggled to get his own seat belt undone before he was strangled to death.

"Cat, wait. I need to get out," he protested as his friend dragged him out of the SUV.

The tall, dark haired woman threw herself into his arms and almost crushed his ribs hugging him. "I'm so glad you're here. It's starting to feel real."

Jensen embraced her just as tightly. "I'll get excited when we get to Lukla and start trekking into Base Camp."

Cat slugged him. "You're so jaded. Now where's your wonderful partner?"

"Sitting in the back with your beautiful daughter." Jensen pointed to the back passenger door of the vehicle.

"Great. I'll sit back there with them and we can chat on the way to the restaurant." Cat pecked him on the cheek before she climbed into the back with Pamela and Toby.

Jigger chuckled at Jensen's expression. "There are days when she's like a hurricane, dude, and all you can do is endure the whirlwind that is Cat."

When they piled back in, Cat and Toby started talking up a storm around little interruptions by Pamela, who was telling her mother about her day. Jigger shot Jensen an amused glance.

"It's like they're long lost siblings," he muttered and Jigger nodded.

Jensen loved how much Toby and Cat adored each other. It meant a lot to him that his two best friends liked the man he loved. Of course, he wished Toby's best friend liked him more, but there was nothing he could about that. Simpson would believe what he chose to believe about Jensen and all he could do to prove him wrong was to keep returning from these trips.

"Oh my God, really?"

They both winced at the volume and shrillness of Cat's voice. Jensen looked back in time to see her try to hug Toby, but there wasn't any room for her to do that. Toby smirked in Jensen's direction before nodding.

"Yes. In exchange, I want your fried chicken recipe," Toby negotiated.

Cat's head bobbed up and down as though she was one of those bobble head dolls. "Of course. I'll show you how to make it while you're here."

"Great." Toby shot Jensen a smug smile.

"Woo-hoo! We get fried chicken." Jigger gave Jensen a fist bump. "Haven't had that in a while."

"I thought it would take a million bucks or something to pry that out of you. What is he bribing you with to get that recipe?" Jensen asked.

Cat mimed zipping her lips shut then locking it before throwing the key over her shoulder. "I'm not going to tell. It's a deal between Toby and me."

Jensen pursed his lips and rolled his eyes. "Fine. Be that way."

Jigger pulled into the parking lot of the restaurant. After piling out, they made their way inside then found a table. The waitress waved at them, showing she'd seen them. When she was done with the couple she'd been talking to, she brought over menus.

"How are you doing?" She greeted Jigger and Cat then patted Pamela on the head.

"We're fine, Sally. You remember Jensen Brockhoff, our climbing buddy?" Cat nodded toward him.

"Of course. Good to see you again, Jensen. And who is this handsome man?" She flashed a flirty smile at Toby.

"This is Toby Schwartzel, Jensen's partner."

Jensen saw her inhale sharply and he thought Jigger had crushed her hopes. He didn't say anything, not wanting to get Sally upset, though she never seemed to be disgusted by him.

"Figures," she muttered. Then she pulled out her pad. "What can I get you all to drink?"

Iced tea and coffee were ordered around the table since Cat and Jigger didn't drink either. Jensen studied the menu, even though he knew what he wanted. Toby looked everything over and Jensen wondered what he thought of the choices. They hadn't come to this place the last time they'd visited Wyoming.

The selection was simple and rustic—nothing gourmet. He knew Toby wouldn't care. He wasn't a snob about his food or where he lived or anything like that. It was just Toby might not have seen some of the meals being offered.

"Are you ready to order?" Sally asked after she delivered their drinks.

"What do you recommend?" Toby gave her a smile and Jensen saw her fall under his spell.

His lover had a way of getting people to like him, but Jensen knew it was part of Toby's charm. He was a nice guy to begin with.

"Our meatloaf is probably the best in the county," Sally told him.

"Then I'll have that." Toby handed her his menu. "What comes with it?"

"Mashed potatoes with gravy and a salad. What kind of dressing do you want?"

"Ranch."

She turned to the rest of them to get what they wanted, plus a hot dog for Pamela. Once she was gone, Toby turned to look at Cat.

"Are you excited about going to Nepal?"

Cat nodded. "Oh yes. Not just to climb, but to be able to see the monasteries and the scenery. I've heard the people there are wonderful and friendly."

"I want to climb, but I want to see the mountain. If I don't make the summit, I can still stare up at Everest and see how amazing it is." Jensen wiped his hands on his thighs as he spoke.

Toby glanced at Jigger. "What are you looking forward to when you get to Nepal?"

"Summiting Everest, man. There's no other reason to go there. What's in Nepal but the highest mountain in the world?" Jigger eyed Toby as though he were stupid.

Jensen and Cat laughed at Jigger's response. For him, there was no other reason to go there—just like there was no other reason to go to Pakistan except to climb K2, or to go to Japan except Mount Fuji. Jigger was about the mountains, nothing else.

Toby shook his head. "Maybe when you get back from your expedition, we can take a couple weeks and go to Australia, Jensen. I'd love to dive on the Great Barrier Reef with you."

"Ooh...you could go to the Guadalupe Islands and cage dive with Great White sharks. There are charters that will take you out," Jigger suggested.

Jensen expected Toby to say no, but he seemed intrigued. At the thought of swimming with thousand pound eating machines, Jensen's heart literally skipped a beat. He wasn't sure he trusted the cages to keep them safe.

"That might be an adventure for us to take after your climbing days are over," Toby told him.

"Umm...yeah. Maybe several years after I'm done climbing," Jensen hedged.

The three of them stared at him and Cat grinned. She leaned over to poke him in the side.

"You aren't afraid of the water, are you?"

He glared at her. "I've been swimming with you before, Cat. Of course, I'm not afraid of the water."

"Then you must be afraid of the sharks. You'll be in a big cage, for goodness' sake. They can't attack you in there," Jigger pointed out.

He swallowed then Toby took his hand in his. Meeting Toby's understanding gaze, Jensen said, "I know that, Jigger, but somehow knowing that it's a few bars of steel to keep me from being eaten by a dinosaur doesn't fill me with confidence."

"Dino?" Pamela perked up when she heard one of her favorite words.

Cat pulled out a stuffed T-Rex from the bag she'd carried into the restaurant then handed it to the little girl, who proceeded to make roaring noises while shoving the animal all around the table.

"So we know one thing you're afraid of." Jigger propped his head on his hand. "That's good. I thought you were a fearless man."

"There are a lot of things that scare me. Hell, I'm scare sh…witless every time we're on the side of a rock wall, hanging hundreds of feet in the air with only some rope and a piece of metal to keep us from plunging to our deaths. I was scared to death when I saw Toby the first time after being gone for six years," he confessed.

Toby tightened his grip on Jensen's hand, bringing his complete attention to him. Jensen licked his lips and Toby gave him an encouraging smile.

"I was so afraid you wouldn't let me talk to you. That you'd tell me to leave the instant you saw me and would never allow me to tell you the reasons why I left. I was prepared to do whatever I needed to do to convince you to forgive me. Somehow Fate smiled on me because you did, and I got a chance to be with the only person I will love forever." Jensen closed his eyes when Cat and Jigger applauded his heartfelt admission.

"Ignore them," Toby whispered. "I'm glad you showed up at my apartment. I knew you'd have stuck around, badgering me until I broke down and let you in. Maybe I should've made you suffer more or grovel more, but I couldn't. I loved you before you left, and I thought I hated you while you were gone. Yet the moment I saw you in that bar, I realized I'd been lying to myself. I still loved you and I'll always love you, no matter how many times you leave me."

"Shouldn't one of you be getting on a knee and offering the other one a ring?" Cat jumped in. They frowned at her and she held up her hands. "I'm just saying. Those sounded like proposals to me."

Toby rolled his eyes and Jensen snorted in disgust.

"It's legal where you live, isn't it?" Jigger tapped his fingers on the table. "Hell, it's legal here. You could do a short ceremony here before you head home, Toby. Then have your mom plan a big one for when Jensen gets back from Everest. It could be a big celebration."

Chapter Seven

*Love is friendship that has caught fire. It is quiet
understanding, mutual confidence, sharing and forgiving.
It is loyalty through good and bad times. It settles for less
than perfection and makes allowances for human
weaknesses.*

— Ann Landers

Toby had a feeling that Jigger had been joking at the
restaurant, yet he couldn't get the thought of marrying
Jensen out of his head. What their friends had
suggested seemed like a good idea. In a way, he wanted
Jensen wearing his ring when he went to Everest. He
had a strange feeling it would give him a bigger
incentive to come home — not that he didn't have one
already.

Later that night, he slipped from Jensen's trailer and
wandered across the yard to Cat and Jigger's house.
They always left the back door unlocked in case Toby
or Jensen wanted a midnight snack — or to use the

bathroom. Toby took care of that problem then went to the kitchen to raid the refrigerator.

"Did we freak you out earlier talking about marriage?" Cat spoke from where she stood in the doorway leading to their rooms.

He'd heard her walk in, so when she voiced her question, he wasn't surprised. Turning, he held up a bottle of apple juice. "You want something to drink?"

"Sure. At least it's not coffee or soda. Caffeine this late at night gives me nightmares." She padded over to the cupboard to get two glasses down. "Why don't you grab the leftover pie? We can finish that."

Toby did as she said, carrying everything to the table where she met him with the glasses and forks.

"Are you panicking about the idea of marrying Jensen?"

He shook his head. "No. Jensen spoke about us getting married and adopting children before we came out here. I told him we'd talk about all of that once he was done climbing. It didn't seem fair to a child to have one of their parents gone half the time on dangerous adventures."

Cat nodded. "I know. That's why I'm done after Everest. I don't want to leave Pamela an orphan if something bad were to happen to both of us during a climb. I mean, we'll still go out, but not to the high altitude mountains. Just stick to the States."

"I'm glad." He took a bite of the lemon meringue pie then swallowed before he continued, "I know it's none of my business how you live your life. I just can't help but think that Pamela would lose out on not knowing you and Jigger if you were to die before she grew up."

"You know that Jensen is her guardian, right? It's all legal and everything. If something happens to us, you and him will get her to raise." Cat giggled. "Not that I want anything bad to happen to us either, but I have to admit, I think that experience could turn out rather funny for you both."

Toby shook his head. "She might end up scarred for life if we had to raise her."

Cat tilted her head as she looked at him then pointed her fork at him. "You're thinking about getting married here before you go home, aren't you?"

He dropped his gaze to the pile of meringue in front of him. "Is it crazy to want to have one more thing to tie Jensen to me?"

She shook her head. "Oh honey. No, it isn't crazy, though I have to say, Jensen doesn't need a ring or a wedding vow to bring him back to you. You have his heart and, without it, he's half a man. The last couple of climbs we've done together, he always seemed to be looking home instead of ahead, and when that happens, it's only a matter of time before a climber calls it quits."

"I don't want him to change or stop doing what he loves," Toby protested. "I simply want him to remember me when the siren winds of the mountains start luring him away. I want to give him a home he wants to return to. I never want him to feel obligated to come back."

"He doesn't. I've never seen him so eager to get back to the States. Before you reconciled, he loved to hang out with the other climbers, telling tall tales about some of their most harrowing climbs. Now we get off the mountain and he's trying to figure out how soon he can get a flight out." Cat chuckled. "I never thought I'd see the day, but it's not a bad thing. You've become his lodestone, Toby, drawing him to you. You are his magnetic North and always will be."

Toby relaxed into his chair, put at ease by Cat's words. "So do you think we could pull off a wedding in only four days? I don't know anything about the laws around here. How long does it take to get a marriage license granted in Wyoming?"

"We can check on it first thing tomorrow. Jigger and I didn't get married here, so I don't know the laws." Cat clapped her hands in joy. "I can't believe this. We'll have to go shopping for rings as well."

"Don't get too carried away. I just want a little ceremony without any fuss, maybe even at the court house if we can't find a minister to do it." Toby cleared his throat. "Of course, Jensen might not want to do it so soon. He might want to wait until he gets back from your trip."

Cat flapped her hands at him. "That's crazy talk. Of course, he'll want to marry you as soon as he can. If he's already mentioned the possibility to you, then it's been in his head for a while. You can talk to him in the morning and we can get the ball rolling."

"Actually he doesn't have to wait until morning."

Toby started when Jensen appeared in the doorway from the back yard. He met his lover's eyes and saw tears in them. After jumping to his feet, Toby raced over to cradle Jensen's face in hands.

"Why are you crying? Don't you want to get married? We don't have to do it right now. We can wait until you're ready," Toby rattled on, so worried that Jensen didn't want to marry him.

Jensen silenced him with a kiss, pulling him tight against his body. Toby whimpered as all the love Jensen felt for him became apparent as they embraced. Finally, when he didn't have any more air in his lungs, he eased a few inches away, but Jensen rested his forehead against Toby's.

"Never think that I don't want to marry you, Toby Schwartzel. I have loved you for years and nothing would make me happier than to say 'I do' to you in front of a minister. I want it legal. I'll rest easier, knowing you have my ring on your finger while I'm gone." Jensen lifted the corner of his mouth in a slight self-derogatory expression. "I'm afraid you'll come to your senses and let someone else sweep you off your feet while I'm away. But it's harder to get rid of a husband than it is a boyfriend."

Toby pinched Jensen's side. "I wouldn't do that to you."

Jensen rubbed his abused flesh. "I know that, but I can't help thinking it once in a while."

"All right, you two. Get over here and help me finish this pie. We'll talk about what we need to do. I have the rest of the week off, so I can go with you to the courthouse in the morning. We'll see what hoops you need to jump through to apply for a marriage license. I'll send Jigger to the church down the road from here. They seem like nice people and I know there are a few gay couples that go there. The minister shouldn't be opposed to performing a wedding." Cat started to click off things they needed to do.

Keeping Toby's hand in his, Jensen led the way back to the table where Toby shared his fork with him. Toby couldn't believe what they were about to do. He would have to call his mom in the morning and tell her. She wasn't going to be happy, but if he explained that they would have a bigger one after Jensen returned, she might forgive them.

"Do you want to call your parents?" he asked Jensen during a lull in Cat's organizing.

Shaking his head, Jensen said, "They couldn't be bothered to visit or call me since I left for boarding school. I don't need them to know anything about me. Your family, Cat, Jigger, and Pamela will be enough, though your mom might not be thrilled about us rushing this."

"At least they don't have worry that you're pregnant," Cat quipped and burst out laughing when they glared at her. "Oh come on. That was funny."

Toby leaned against Jensen's shoulder. "Your friends are crazy," he announced to Jensen.

"Probably all those brain cells they've lost while climbing at high altitudes without oxygen," Jensen conceded.

Cat huffed at them, but went back to working out all the things they needed to do to get even a small ceremony done in time. Toby's heart gave a little flutter of joy. By the time he flew home to Connecticut, he was going to be Toby Schwartzel-Brockhoff. If he wasn't the only Schwartzel boy, he wouldn't even consider hyphenating his name, but he'd do it out of respect for his dad.

"I'm going to change my last name to Schwartzel," Jensen spoke up, obviously thinking about the same thing as Toby.

He turned to face Jensen. "Are you sure? Aren't you an only son like me?"

Jensen nodded. "Yeah, but my name doesn't mean anything to me. I certainly don't have any respect — or connection — to it, not like you have to yours. Plus I like your family."

"My mom is going to be over the moon about this," Toby confessed. "You're going to have to prepare for a big gathering when you get home in June. You'll get to meet the extended family and Dad will be bragging about your trip."

The look of joy on Jensen's face made Toby seriously think about what it must have been like for Jensen to be totally ignored his entire life. Where Toby might have rolled his eyes and been amused by his father's bragging, Jensen was going to love it.

"I'll make sure to bring back some souvenirs for them." Jensen took a bite of the pie and made a face. "How can you guys like this sour shit?"

"It's not that bad," Cat said before taking a bite. "Do you want a little party here? I know there are some of the other guys who are going on our trip in the area. They'd love a reason to get together before we have to start training."

Toby met Jensen's questioning gaze. "It's up to you. I'm fine with a party or just the five of us having a nice dinner in Laramie. They're your friends."

Jensen snorted. "I wouldn't call them friends. They're more acquaintances than anything else. You know what, Cat? I would love it just being the five of us. We can get a really nice dinner then Toby and I'll get a hotel room for the night."

"Why would we do that when we've got the trailer?" Toby thought he knew why, but he wanted to see what Jensen's reason was.

"I'm not going to have our wedding night be in that ratty old trailer, Toby. I mean, it's fine for a normal night, but not something special like that." Jensen looked indignant.

He threw himself into Jensen's arms, practically sitting on his lap at the table. "I wouldn't care if we stayed in a yurt, as long as I was married to you."

Jensen kissed him while Cat cackled in the background. When they were done, he turned to look at her. "What's so funny?"

"Have you ever stayed in a yurt?"

Toby shook his head. "Of course not. There aren't a lot of those around New York or Connecticut, for that matter."

"I have a friend in Colorado who lives in one. Next summer you can come out here and we'll go visit him. You can get a taste of living in a yurt, then you'll think that trailer is a luxurious penthouse suite." Cat paused then continued, "Or maybe you'll love it and sell your nice house on the East Coast to move into one."

"Not going to happen," Jensen interrupted. "I get my full of living in a tent while on these climbing trips. I don't want to come home to live in one here."

Cat applauded. "Good point."

Toby started to climb off Jensen's lap, but Jensen wouldn't let him. They snuggled together while cleaning up the last bites. When they were done, they helped Cat wash up before heading back out to the trailer.

Once there, Toby stripped off his clothes then climbed under the blankets and shivered. Even with the heater on, the bedroom was cold. He held out his hand to Jensen.

"Get under here with me. I need your body heat," he whined.

Jensen stripped as well before crawling in next to him. Toby entwined his arms and legs around Jensen, getting as close to him as possible. Their cocks bumped and he groaned. Rolling on to his back, he drew Jensen with him.

Pressing his lips to Jensen's ear, Toby whispered, "Make love to me."

He was still stretched from earlier that night, so Jensen pressed his lube-covered erection slowly into Toby's channel. Toby bit his bottom lip at the pressure, but didn't break eye contact with Jensen.

Both of them froze when Jensen was all the way in. Toby cradled Jensen's face in his hands.

"I love you, Jensen Brockhoff, and in a day or two, you and I will be married. We will belong to each other in the eyes of God and the law. No one can take this away from us, no matter what happens in the future."

Jensen blinked and Toby could've sworn there were tears in his lover's eyes as Jensen took a breath before saying, "I love you more than anything else in this world, Toby Schwartzel. I'm going to put a ring on your finger, so everyone know how lucky I am to have you as mine."

With their vows said in the quiet darkness around them, Toby lifted his hips just a little to let Jensen know he could move. Slow and gentle strokes in and out. There was no rush or urgency in their love making right then. It was just moments spent feeling each other and imprinting the sound of Jensen's breath washing over Toby's ear and the scrape of the stubble on Jensen's chin against Toby's neck.

It felt as if it was their wedding night right there in the privacy of this rundown trailer Jensen had lived in for six years while trying to become a better man for Toby. Yet Toby would've told him back then — if Jensen had given him a chance — that Jensen was perfect.

Rocking into each thrust, Toby placed kisses along Jensen's jaw, throat and chest, sucking small marks up at random spots. He wasn't sure how long they lay there, locked together in their beautiful carnal dance, but when his climax hit him, it was a complete surprise.

"Jensen!" He cried out, cum spurting from his cock.

His shuddering and undulating must have pushed Jensen over the edge because it was only a few seconds later that Jensen came, filling his ass and yelling his name as he did so. He moaned as Jensen flopped to the side and slid out of his body.

Being gathered into Jensen's arms as though his lover couldn't stand to be even an inch away from him brought a smile to Toby's face. He didn't complain about the cooling strings of cum that were going to stick them together in the morning. Right then, he didn't think that was a bad thing.

Chapter Eight

Friends can help each other. A true friend is someone who lets you have total freedom to be yourself – and especially to feel. Or, not feel. Whatever you happen to be feeling at the moment is fine with them. That's what real love amounts to – letting a person be what he really is.

– Jim Morrison

Jensen rubbed his sweaty palms on his shirt before turning to look at Jigger. His friend grinned.

"Getting nervous?"

"Yes. It's stupid to be nervous about this. It's not like Toby's going to back out or run away. He's as committed to this relationship as I am." He cleared his throat. "It's just..."

"It's a major step. Sure, moving in together was a big one, but you were willing to do it because Toby wanted you living with him. It gave you a base to build from, more than the trailer in my backyard." Jigger tweaked Jensen's collar. "This means Toby really is going to keep you. There's no walking away from this, not without a lot of damage on both sides."

Stiffening, he glared at Jigger. "I'm not going to walk away. Even if we never got married, I wasn't going to abandon him again."

Jigger tapped his cheek. "I know that and Toby knows that as well, but this helps heal the scar you inflicted all those years ago. You're letting him bind you to him with rings and vows."

"I can't believe how fast this is all happening," he muttered as he paced in the small room behind the pulpit at the little country church Cat had told him about three days ago.

They'd gone to the Laramie County courthouse to apply for a marriage license. Shockingly there wasn't a waiting period. Jensen had his birth certificate with him, but they needed Toby's mother to overnight a copy of Toby's before they could get a license. It only took an extra day and it gave them time to plan the rest of the small ceremony.

After that, they'd gone ring shopping. There wasn't a huge selection of jewelry shops in the town, but neither one of them wanted anything fancy or expensive. Jensen pulled the simple platinum band out of his pocket. The date and his name had been engraved on the one he held. Toby had the one with his own name on it to give to Jensen during the ceremony.

"I forgot to ask you how Toby's parents took the news?" Jigger asked, probably trying to take Jensen's mind off his upcoming nuptials.

"I thought Toby lost hearing in his right ear from her screaming. Then she started crying and his dad came on to try and figure out why his wife was having a meltdown." He grinned at the happiness the Schwartzels had expressed at him becoming their son-in-law. "They were both really excited about it. They wanted us to wait until tomorrow so they could fly out, but Toby promised we'd have a big ceremony and reception in August when I've recovered from the Everest climb."

Jigger laughed. "Better reception than I got when Cat took me home to meet her dad. When he found out I used to be in a rock band, he almost lost it. Then once he realized which one it was, I thought he was going throw me out of the house. He chewed Cat out about being deceived by a sex fiend like me. It was bad enough that she'd obviously slept with me, but to believe that I actually wanted to marry her was crazy."

Jensen cringed. "He didn't care that you could take care of her financially? That she wouldn't have to work another day in her life, if she didn't want to? All he saw was the tattoos, long hair and bad reputation, huh?"

"Yep." Jigger took a lock of his long hair in his fingers and tugged lightly. "I had planned on cutting it before we went, but she told me not to—that if her father couldn't see what a wonderful man I was underneath all the ink and long hair, then he was the one at fault. Not me."

"The more stories you guys tell me about him, the more I'm glad I've never met him."

"He's a winner, that's for sure. It's awesome that Toby's family really seems to have taken to you. Be glad about that."

And he was *very* glad. Before he could say anything else, the door opened and the minister peeked in, her thin face wreathed in a bright smile.

"Are you ready in here?"

"God, yes." Jensen winced. "Sorry."

Her laugh was high and joyous. "Son, I don't think He'll mind, not when we're celebrating such a marvelous occasion here today."

Jigger clapped him on the shoulder. "Let's go get you married, man."

Taking a deep breath then releasing it slowly, Jensen nodded. He followed his best friend and the minister out to stand in front of the altar. He shot a quick glance up at the stained glass cross hanging in the large picture window.

At one time, Jensen hadn't believed in God—or a higher spirit. He'd believed man was lost and alone on the planet. Then he'd climbed his first mountain and stood at the top. He'd looked out over the world, realizing that God wasn't a faraway entity ignoring the creatures He'd brought into being. God was everywhere. He existed in the air Jensen breathed and the water he drank. God was in the rocks under his feet and the clouds sweeping across the blue sky. Jensen had prayed at that moment, thanking God for keeping him alive long enough to realize how much he wanted to live.

Music started and as the opening chords from k.d. Lang's version of *Hallelujah* drifted through the almost empty church, he turned to see Toby walking down the aisle toward him. Watching the man he loved make his way to him, Jensen sent another prayer upward, promising to love him forever and thanking God for convincing Toby to give him another chance.

For Jensen, Toby's heart was where God really lived. The loving spirit he showed to Jensen every day was the finest example of God existing that Jensen had ever seen—even more than the beautiful mountains he climbed.

He held out his hand when Toby got close to him. The dazzling smile Toby bestowed on him eased Jensen's heart. He relaxed. This ceremony was a small detail that wouldn't change anything in the grand scheme of their lives.

Toby gripped his hand tightly as he stepped up next to him. Jensen couldn't resist, so he leaned forward to place a soft kiss on Toby's cheek. The minister cleared her throat and they turned to look at her.

"I'm so glad that I'm finally able to do this," she announced. "Even if it's the smallest wedding I've seen in my many years of ministering."

Jensen glanced over his shoulder to where Jigger and Cat stood, holding Pamela in their arms. They were his family and while it might not have been fair to Toby to have no one here, Jensen knew Toby wasn't too upset about it.

Suddenly the door opened at the back of the sanctuary and three people stepped in. Toby gasped when they got closer and they saw it was Toby's parents and Simpson. Toby's mom rushed up to them, throwing her arms around them.

"We couldn't let you get married without us," she said, kissing them each on the cheek.

"After I talked to you yesterday, I got us all plane tickets out here. I talked to Brockhoff about the time and everything." Simpson slapped Toby on the back then shook Jensen's hand. "Thanks for making it as late as you could."

Toby whirled to look at him. "Is this why you said we had to have it in the afternoon? Not some silly climbing tradition?"

Shrugging, Jensen grinned. "There might be some kind of tradition about weddings in the climbing community, but I don't know them. I just knew we had to do this as late as we could so they had a chance to get here. Almost didn't make it."

"Sorry about that," Simpson said. "Got a little lost on the way out of Laramie."

Toby's dad hugged them both before turning to greet the minister. "Sorry to interrupt, ma'am."

"It's no problem. I'm happy to see there's family here for both of you." She motioned for Toby's parents and Simpson to take their seats. "Like I started to say, it's been a long time coming, but now I can finally marry all couples—no matter their sex—in the eyes of our loving God."

Jensen held Toby's hand through the entire ceremony. He trembled while he slid the band on Toby's ring finger then didn't feel so bad when he saw that Toby was doing the same. He spoke his vows in a loud firm voice, not wanting anyone to think he had any hesitation about this wedding—or his love for this man.

At the end, the minister smiled at both of them. "'A new commandment I give you—Love one another. As I have loved you, so you must love one another.' That was Jesus' commandment to us and it's the only bit of advice I'll give you today. Jesus loves us with all our faults and mistakes. You must try to keep that same kind of love for each other. If you do, your lives will be filled with such incredible joy. Now you may kiss and start your new life together."

Jensen encircled Toby's waist before pulling him near. He stared down into his husband's eyes, seeing the tears glimmering in them. Bending, he pressed his lips to Toby's cheeks and claimed those tears as his. Then he took a quick kiss from Toby.

A soft sob escaped from Toby as he wrapped his arms around Jensen's neck. He hid his face against Jensen's chest, obviously trying to get his feelings under control. Jensen whispered nonsensical words while rubbing Toby's back.

Once Toby got himself back together, they stepped apart then turned to face the six people waiting for them.

"Everyone, may I introduce Mr. and Mr. Toby and Jensen Schwartzel," the minister announced.

"Oh my," Toby's mom gasped and Toby's dad wiped a tear from his cheek.

"So pretty," Pamela cried, as she tried to grab the flame of the flickering candle on the altar.

"No, honey. You can't touch that. Why don't we go give Uncle Toby and Uncle Jensen hugs?" Cat brought the little girl to them.

They got wet kisses from Pamela and warm hugs from Jigger and Cat.

Jensen grasped Simpson's hand and shook it. "Thanks for getting them out here," he told him. "I know you and I aren't ever going to be best friends, but I do appreciate the effort it took."

"It was your plan, man. I just put it in motion." Simpson grimaced. "You're right about us, but you know what? We don't have to be as long as we accept that we have something in common."

"What's that?" Jensen turned to check where Toby was.

"We'll both do whatever we have to do to keep Toby from getting hurt."

Jensen met Simpson's intense gaze. "I'll never hurt Toby again, Simpson. I promised him that when he took me back."

Simpson nodded before moving on to introduce himself to Jigger and Cat. There was none of the usual fawning from people when they realized who Jigger was. Jensen shouldn't have been surprised. He figured Simpson had probably done a background check on both of them the instant Jensen had reappeared. The man wasn't taking any chances with Toby. He was like an overly protective older brother.

"Jensen honey, come here." Toby's mom gestured for him to join her where she stood with Toby and the others.

He strolled over and got enveloped by another hug. He breathed in her simple perfume of lavender and vanilla. It certainly beat the expensive scents his mother wore.

"I can't believe you took our last name." She stepped back to look up at him.

Lifting one shoulder, he said, "I'm not attached to my last name, Mrs. Schwartzel. It didn't make sense to make Toby change his or hyphenate it when I could just change mine."

"Please call me Mom — or Nancy, if you can't call me that yet." She tucked her hand in the crook of his arm. "But what will your parents say when you tell them?"

Jensen licked his lips as he tried to think of a way not to have to talk about his family. Not on such a wonderful day as this. Yet he knew she wouldn't let it go. Mom could be a bulldog when it came to dig out the truth.

"Well, Mom."

She beamed at him and Toby winked at him from where he stood between Simpson and Jigger, holding Pamela.

"I haven't spoken to my parents in years. I have no idea how they'll react because I don't plan on telling them." It was blunt, but it was how he felt about the whole situation. They'd never made any effort to contact him. He wasn't going to ruin the memories of his wedding by calling his folks and finding out they didn't care one whit about him.

"Oh honey." She hugged his arm. "Did they throw you out because you were gay?"

"Mom," Toby interjected. "There are other reasons why people don't talk to their parents."

She flapped her hand at him. Jensen started moving toward the door. They'd paid the minister before the ceremony, plus they'd given a generous donation to the church. They had reservations at the nicest restaurant in Laramie and Jensen wanted to head over there.

"My parents ignored me until I was sixteen then they sent me off to boarding school. I think that's when they forgot about me. They never came to any of my games or any of my other school events, except my graduation. I got a letter from my dad telling me my tuition to Harvard was paid for, so when I got accepted there, that's where I went." He shrugged. "After that, I've had no contact with either of them. I'm not even sure they're still alive."

"Of course they are, or else you'd get contacted by lawyers," Simpson spoke up. "You're an only child, right?"

He didn't understand this fascination with his family. "Yes. All right. Simpson, why don't you follow us to the restaurant?"

Jensen got everyone sorted out between the two vehicles before they were underway to supper. He settled in the backseat with Toby and Pamela, entertaining her while holding Toby's hand.

Toby whispered, "I'm sorry about my mom. She's concerned for you. Mom hates when people aren't treated well. And she loved it that you called her Mom."

"I just don't see the point of rehashing my family history. None of that matters any more. I have my family right here. You. These three. Your parents and siblings. Heck, even Simpson is part of it." Jensen tilted his head at Jigger and Cat. "Maybe someday we'll have kids to add to it."

"Oh we'll have kids," Toby swore.

His heart jumped. All Jensen knew about raising kids was not to do what his parents had done. He had a feeling that would be a good rule to follow when they added children to their lives.

Chapter Nine

...but attempting to climb Everest is an intrinsically irrational act – a triumph of desire over sensibility. Any person who would seriously consider it is almost by definition beyond the sway of reasoned argument.

– Jon Krakauer, Into Thin Air

"We got here all right and met up with the guides from the company. We're going to hang here in Katmandu for a day while the rest of the group comes in. Once we're all here, we'll take a prop jet out to Lukla before we trek up to Base Camp," Jensen told Toby over the phone. He leaned against the wall in the room he was sharing with Jigger and Cat.

"Did all your stuff make it over there okay?" Toby sounded relieved that they'd completed the first step of their journey without incident.

He chuckled. "Yeah. It's stored with the rest of the expedition's stuff or we wouldn't fit into our room."

Toby laughed. "You did take a lot of stuff."

Jensen nodded, even though Toby couldn't see him. "There was a lot, but you know it was for three people. Thank God, I don't have to carry it all. Most of it will be carried up to Base Camp by yak, with our Sherpas keeping an eye on it."

"Will you be able to keep in touch when you get there?" The hesitation in Toby's voice told Jensen he was afraid of seeming too needy.

"As long as the weather is good, we should be able to make some calls while there, plus I'll write you a letter every night I can. I won't be able to mail them to you, but it'll give you something to read when I get home."

He'd packed several notebooks, planning on keeping a journal about his climb. It would be even nicer to turn the entries into letters to Toby. Maybe it would help Toby connect with the trip.

"I'd love to read them." Toby yawned. "I better get to bed."

"Sorry about the late call," he apologized.

Toby grunted. "No. Don't worry about it. Call me whenever you get the chance. I promise I'll answer, even if I'm at work. I'll just explain that my husband is climbing Everest. They'll all be suitably impressed."

Laughing, Jensen looked up to see Jigger peer around the door then motion to him to come on. "Hey love, I have to go. Have a meeting with the guides to decide strategy on the mountain. I'll call as soon as I can tomorrow."

"All right. I love you. Have fun and please be safe."

"I love you too, Toby."

Toby ended the call first and Jensen slid his phone in his jacket pocket. He scrubbed his hand over his hair as he went to join Jigger out in the hallway. Cat stood a little bit away, chatting with one of the other female climbers going out with them on this expedition.

"Toby doing okay?" Jigger asked while pushing himself off the wall.

"Yeah. I'm glad we were able to get a layover in New York so I could see him before we flew here." He ran his thumb over the wide band on his ring finger. He'd gotten into the habit of doing that after Toby had flown home. It soothed him.

"Good." Jigger gathered the others and led the way downstairs to one of the conference rooms in the hotel where their guides were waiting for them.

* * * *

Two days later, Jensen stepped off the plane in Lukla, fighting the urge to drop to his knees and kiss the runaway. He'd heard stories about how scary flying in and out of Lukla could be, but he'd thought they were exaggerated. The pilots had to be experienced and bloody fearless to guide their planes into the village. There was a very small margin for error with the short runway and sharp drop off at the end of it. Hell, if the plane didn't get off the ground on takeoff — or stop soon enough on landing — the aircraft and its passengers could careen into an unforgiving obstacle.

Jensen stopped to glance around, mostly to quit trembling, but also to stare at some of the most beautiful scenery he'd ever seen. Mountains covered with green forest surrounded Lukla. Luckily the weather was good today, so the sky was clear. Yet fog clung to the uppermost parts of the trees, giving the scenery a haunted feel, as though the ghosts of the long dead gathered among them.

He carried his backpack across the small tarmac, following his guides to the Everest Summit Lodge where they were staying for the night. Jigger and Cat were right behind him. The outside of the lodge was built with native stone and the sharp angled roof peaks added the rustic flare Jensen had been hoping for. The hardwood floors and wood paneled walls gleamed. It looked like a great deal of care went into making the lodge beautiful for the trekkers who stayed there. There was a very laid-back feel to the place. Jensen relaxed, soaking up the peacefulness. He wished he could bottle it and take some with him when they left for Base camp, because he knew he wasn't going to find much once they were up on the mountain.

After they got their rooms and dumped their bags, they went down to get something to eat since their flight was the last one in from Katmandu at three-thirty in the afternoon.

When they were seated and had gotten their tea, Jensen looked at his friends and exhaled. "Thank God Toby isn't with us. I think he would've lost his mind if he had to fly into this airport."

"I know. Holy shit! You have to be crazy or a very competent pilot to land and take off here." Jigger shook his head. "Just think… We get to do that on our way back home."

"Oh come on, mate. It wasn't that bad." Rodney, one of their guides, said, as he joined them at their table. Rodney wasn't the head guide, but he'd been to Everest six times and had experience with other high altitude climbs.

All the guides with the expedition had solid reputations in the climbing community, which was why they'd chosen to go with them. Yet Jensen wondered if all that high altitude climbing had destroyed more brain cells than Rodney could afford to lose.

"Maybe if I took that flight on a regular basis, I'd get used to it, but then again, maybe not." Jensen sipped his tea. "When do we head out?"

"The Sherpas will be taking the yaks out tomorrow around four in the morning. We'll leave a little later heading to Namche Baazar. It'll take us two days to reach it. It's at eleven thousand two hundred and ninety feet. We'll rest there for a day while getting acclimatized." Rodney scratched his chin. "Then hike another two days to Dingboche at thirteen thousand nine hundred and eighty feet. Another rest day before we head out for Base Camp. It'll take another two days for us to reach that."

"Base Camp is at seventeen thousand five hundred and ninety-eight feet right?" Jigger pulled out the beat-up leather journal he'd carried on all his climbs then flipped through the pages to get where he'd written down the stats for Everest.

"Right, man. A week to get there. It's slow, but it'll help get you used to the altitude around here. I've had altitude sickness before and it sucks. Plus, you don't want to cut your trip short by rushing it." Rodney waved to some of the other climbers. "I heard this is your last one, Cat."

She nodded. "Yes. We have a daughter, and I just don't have the drive to go any more. Don't want to make her an orphan either."

Rodney nodded as he pulled a wallet from his back pocket. "I got two little girls myself. Hate to leave them every season, but it's the only way I can climb and get paid for it."

He showed the pictures around and Jensen agreed they were cute.

"You don't have kids, do you, Brockhoff?" Rodney eyed him then noticed the ring on his finger. "But you must have got hitched at some point. Congratulations on that. Thought you were gay though."

"It's Schwartzel now. I am gay, and I live in a state that allows me to get married," he told Rodney. "I got married in February. No, we don't have kids yet. It's something we'll probably think about when I stop climbing."

Rodney chuckled. "Good plan, mate. My wife would rather we had waited as well. First one was a surprise, you know. Oh hey, are you guys in the trip to K2 next year that Ransom's putting together?"

Jigger nodded and they got talking about how that looked to be panning out. Jensen wasn't interested in that at the moment. He was taking Toby's advice and focusing on one trip at a time. No need to get excited about K2 when he still had to summit Everest.

He'd carried his camera down with him, so he took a few candid shots of Jigger, Cat and Rodney before he set it aside when their meals arrived. The staff at the lodge was very courteous and most of them spoke some English.

"Will you all be using supplemental oxygen?" Rodney glanced at them.

"Yes," Jensen answered.

"Awesome. I'll be using it too. I did the summit once in true alpine style, you know. No oxygen except what I could drag into my tired overworked lungs. Just about killed me getting back down, especially when there was a bottleneck at the Step." Rodney grimaced. "I'm pretty sure everyone with our expedition is using oxygen on this climb."

While they ate, they talked about different climbs they'd done and which ones had turned dangerous without warning. Other people wandered by as other expeditions arrived to start their own treks to Base

Camp. Jensen saw a few people he knew, but there seemed to be a lot of strangers.

"How many groups are going out this season?" he asked Rodney as they were getting ready to leave the dining room.

Rodney squinted off into the distance while he thought. "At least eight are heading out now. Hightower wants to be one of the first to try and summit this season. He doesn't like going later because the ladders at the Step get worse for wear after a while, plus they're only maintained through the end of May."

"Right. Still...eight groups with ten to twenty climbers in each group is a lot to shepherded up and down the mountain," he commented as they stepped outside.

"Aye," Rodney agreed. "Some of these guys are going to need their hands held while doing it. Luckily, High made sure our group was filled with experienced climbers. All of you have done at least one or two other eight thousand meter climbs, so you aren't going to get swept up in summit fever. Or I hope you won't."

Jensen shook his head. "I won't. As much as I'd love to have Everest on my résumé, if High—or any of you—tell me to turn back before I hit the top, I will. I have someone expecting me to get home in one piece. I'm not going to disappoint him by going against the advice of my guides. Hell, that's what I'm paying you for."

"Good on you for that, mate." Rodney slapped Jensen's shoulder. "I have to go find High and see what he needs me to do. See you in the morning."

"Bright and early," he muttered as Rodney strolled away.

"Still doesn't feel real, does it?" Jigger stepped up beside Jensen and they stared in the direction of

Everest, the peak shrouded in clouds. Nature hid the massive mountain from the prying eyes of mere humans and rarely deigned to give them even a glimpse of its magnificence.

"No. Probably won't until we get to Base Camp and start climbing. Hell, it might not seem real until we're standing at the summit of Everest, looking down at the rest of the world." Jensen held up his camera. "I'm going to get some pictures around here for Toby and his parents."

"Aren't they your parents too now?" Jigger elbowed him before wandering back inside the lodge.

Jensen didn't reply as he took off to get some good shots of the scenery and the airport. He knew those would scare Toby to death, but as long as Jensen didn't think about it, he'd be able to climb on the airplane when it was time to go home.

* * * *

"Were you able to talk to Jensen today?" Simpson asked, as he flopped down into the chair across from Toby's desk.

He looked up from his computer screens and nodded. "Yes. He called before they started out on the first part of their hike up to Base Camp."

"Why can't they just fly up there?" Simpson grimaced. "I can't imagine hiking anywhere."

Toby chuckled. "You'd only hike if it involved naked women and alcohol."

"Now that would be an entertaining way to go for a walk." Simpson leered.

Rolling his eyes, Toby hit save for the file he'd been working on before giving his friend his full attention. "First of all, there's not enough air up where the camp is to support an airplane. It's even difficult for helicopters to get up there, which is why being med-evac'd out is a big production. Second of all, there is no room to put a landing strip on the side of the mountain. Thirdly, they need to take the week to start getting acclimatized to the lower oxygenated air they'll be breathing. Climbing Everest isn't a cakewalk, Simpson."

Simpson huffed in annoyance. "I know that, Schwartzel. I'm not a complete idiot. So tell me? What's married sex like?"

"Do you want me to tell you all the details?" He wiggled his eyebrows then burst out laughing when Simpson gave him a disgusted look. "You were the one who asked."

"I know. What the hell was I thinking?" Simpson smacked himself in the forehead. "Actually what I wanted to know was, do you feel any different now that you and Brockhoff are married? More secure about him?"

After standing, Toby paced his small office. He was one of the lucky ones who had his own workspace instead of being out in the open area of the bullpen, as they called it. "I don't think I feel any different. I like having this ring on my finger and knowing he wears a matching one. Being married to me isn't going to change things for him except his last name. It's just one more way we've entwined our lives to the point where it'll be very painful for us to break apart."

Simpson shifted in his chair then stuck out his foot to nudge Toby when he went by. Stopping, Toby met his friend's serious gaze.

"You know I'm not Jensen's biggest fan. Probably never will be. I hold grudges like no one's business, but that's not the point. You forgave him and you love him.

I can see how much he loves you every time he looks at you. There won't be any breaking apart this time."

Toby hoped so, and to be honest, he didn't have any doubts that their life together would be forever — or until one of them died. He was just hoping it wouldn't be Jensen in the next month or so while he was away.

"His climbing bothers you, doesn't it?"

When did his best friend get so perceptive?

"Of course it does. Would you be happy if the woman you loved routinely climbed twenty-six thousand foot tall mountains with only ropes and bits of metal to keep her anchored to the rock?" Toby paced again, stuffing his hands in his pockets as he talked. "I guess I don't get why he does it."

"It's a rush and he's a junkie. Brockhoff used to get his high from drugs and alcohol. Now that he can't get it that way, he had to find some other way. I'm guessing that once he gets these last two out of the way, he'll do his best to find a less scary way to get his fix." He chuckled. "Hell, adopt some children. I bet that'll give him the pulse pounding fun he's looking for. From what I've heard, they scare even the most laid-back person."

Toby grinned. "We talked about it, but we're going to wait until after he gets back from his K2 climb. You ready to be an uncle?"

Simpson blinked. "Holy shit! I never thought about that. I will be the world's greatest uncle, you know."

"Yeah. I can't wait to watch you spoil them." Toby glanced at his watch. "Let's go grab something to eat. I have to work late tonight on this new client Abramson gave me."

Simpson jumped to his feet then slung his arm over Toby's shoulders. "I'll buy. I'm getting an amazing bonus for pulling off a huge buy earlier today."

"Good. Then we're going somewhere expensive," Toby teased, making sure he had his phone in case Jensen ended up somewhere he could get a signal and call.

Chapter Ten

*Despite all I've seen and experienced, I still get the same
simple thrill out of glimpsing a tiny patch of snow in a high
mountain gully and feel the same urge to climb towards it.*

– Sir Edmund Hillary

Jensen stumbled into Jigger when his friend stopped
suddenly. "What the hell, Jigger?" he groused as he
grabbed a hold of his shoulder to keep from falling
over. He shifted his backpack to even out the load
again. "Warn a guy next time."

"We're here." Jigger pointed to the city of brightly
colored tents that had seemed to appear out of
nowhere.

Jensen glanced around and couldn't help a little touch
of disappointment from taking hold of him. He'd read
the articles about the trash strewn around the base
camp, left behind from hundreds of expeditions to the
summit. Yet reading about it hadn't prepared him for
the reality. Empty oxygen tanks and broken climbing
equipment lay in heaps, along with discarded food

containers. *No wonder the Nepalese government instituted the rule about climbers having to carry out so many pounds of trash. Humans can't help destroying even this most sacred of mountains.*

Yet when he looked back at the tents, his heart lifted slightly at the sight of the Buddhist prayer flags that decorated several stone cairns. He knew previous climbers had built them in homage of lost comrades and to lift prayers up to the spirits that haunted the slopes and crevasses of Everest. Whether most of the people in camp believed in God or not, they all believed in the mountain as a real entity. Superstition convinced them to place offerings to Everest in the hope for good weather and an uneventful climb. Jensen would be placing his own offering at the foot of the mountain and hope it accepted it.

Even with the intrinsic danger of the climb, the odd cheerfulness of the flags that seemed to point to the summit gave him hope for a successful mission. While the mountain held all the cards, he and the others trusted in their own abilities to weather the roughest patches and triumph in the end.

He laughed. There was always so much optimism at the beginning, but by the time they pushed for the summit, they'd all be worn down by the very object they wanted to conquer.

"Welcome to Everest Base Camp, everyone," Hightower, the head guide for their expedition, called from where he was at the front of the line. "Our tents should be up and ready to go. Follow me and I'll show you where our camp is."

"It looks like half of the other groups are here," Jensen mumbled to Cat as they shuffled along the trail.

"Well, it'll be crazy crowded when the rest arrive," she said.

It was rather noisy with people climbing out of their tents to greet the newcomers. It was obvious that the climbing community was a rather small one, all things considered, especially for those who have attempted — and succeeded at — any eight thousand meter climbs.

Jensen waved to several people he'd met on some other mountain during his adventures, promising he'd catch up with them later after he'd gotten settled in his tent. There would be a lot of tall tales being told that night with maybe a drink or two enjoyed. Not by him though.

"Here's our spot," High told them, gesturing to the collection of tents at the edge of the camp. "We won't be the last ones for long. Get settled in. We're going to rest for two days then we'll start making trips up to set up Camp One. My plan is for us all to try and summit around May twenty-seventh, but we'll see. As every one of you knows, no plan is set in stone or fool-proof, especially when it comes to Everest. The forecast says we should be getting some good climbing weather while we're here, but again, it'll be a crap shoot on whether that happens or not."

Jensen went to find his tent then he set it up next to Cat and Jigger's slightly bigger one. One of the Sherpas came around to check to see if he needed any help, but Jensen sent him to help someone else. He wanted to be as self-sufficient as possible while there. Not that he wasn't going to appreciate the fact that the Sherpas were going to be among the ones breaking the trail and setting the ropes all the way to the summit. They would also be doing most of the hauling from one camp to the next. He had a feeling that the thirty pounds of his personal backpack might be more than enough for him to deal with each day.

He might've been a natural climber — or so Jigger and Cat told him — but he didn't like being in the lead. Over the years, he'd also learned he didn't like climbing with a lot of people. With some of their lower climbs, he'd taken off on his own, rejoining the others later on in the day. He wasn't entirely sure he'd do that on Everest, even if High allowed that to happen.

"Hey, mate, you all good in here?" Rodney stuck his head through the tent flaps and grinned at him.

"Yeah. Do you need help with anything?" He settled his pack and stuff in one of the corners.

"Sure. You can help us set up the main tent. It's where we'll meet each morning to figure out groups and when each one is going out. Plus, you can get info from the outside world there."

Jensen trailed behind Rodney. "I have a satellite phone, so I won't be hanging out trying to make calls."

"Good, because that shit is fucking expensive." Rodney shared a grin with him. "I still use it to call home once in a while. Don't want them to think something happened to me."

"Yeah. That's why I have one as well. It's come in handy for some of the climbs I've done over on this side of the world." Jensen nodded to High when they reached the main part of their section of Base Camp.

"I've recruited more help, High." Rodney motioned to Jensen. "Schwartzel here can get the sat phone set up."

"Schwartzel? I thought your name was Brockhoff," High commented, as he strolled toward them.

High was a big man with broad shoulders and a large booming voice. He was a legend in the climbing world, having made the summits of Everest and K2 three times each, plus he was one of the 'eight-thousanders' — that legendary group of people who had summitted all fourteen of the mountains that were over eight thousand meters high. There weren't that many who had the energy — and luck — to have that happen for them.

People would follow High to the ends of the world because of the sheer confidence he inspired in others. High had never met a person he didn't like, but he had a ferocious temper and if he thought someone was doing something stupid or dangerous, he'd call that person out. Jensen had seen an example of that when they'd climbed Annapurna I three years ago. High had chewed out one of their fellow climbers who had decided to go off on his own. When he'd done that, he'd set off a slight avalanche, that could've have turned into much more but they'd all been lucky that day.

High had been incensed and would've beaten the guy to a bloody pulp if Jensen and one of the other climbers hadn't interceded. He had thrown the guy off the expedition. Jensen didn't know if that climber ever made it to the summit or not. High had gotten the rest of them up there and on that mountain, it had been a major feat, considering the odds were against them the entire way that season.

"Man got married before he came out here. Helluva honeymoon, if you ask me. Leaving his blushing husband back home in… Where do you live exactly?" Rodney stared at Jensen.

"Connecticut," Jensen murmured.

"Ah right." Rodney winked at him before wandering off to help set up a small table and some camp chairs.

"Schwartzel, huh? Wouldn't be that guy you couldn't stop talking about when we climbed Annapurna I, would it?" High motioned for him to come over to him.

Jensen was shocked High remembered anything he might have said during that trip. To many, High came across as very self-absorbed and non-social, but that wasn't it. High was extremely focused and all he really cared about was climbing, making him the perfect guide for expeditions to some of the tallest mountains in the world.

"Yeah, he is." Jensen touched his thumb to his ring then took the cables High handed him.

"Glad to know it worked out for you," High told him before they got caught up in setting up the sat phone and other equipment.

By the time they were done with everything, darkness was starting to fall and Jensen headed out to find Cat and Jigger. When he finally tracked them down, they were visiting with a group of Brits who'd arrived at Base Camp shortly after they had. He was enveloped into the gathering with friendly greetings and offers of a sip or two of whiskey. He turned them down.

It sounded like all the expeditions that had shown up that day were going to stay in camp for two days to rest up from the hike in. There was a South Korean and an Australian contingent that had come up three days before them and they were going to start working their way up to Camp One.

"They set to summit first?" Jensen asked one of the Brits.

"Aye. They'll be breaking the trail for the rest of us. Their Sherpas have already gone up once to set the ropes up to the first camp." The man curled his upper lip. "Not sure about the Koreans though. None of them have done high altitude before. Sounds like this will be the first major climb for all of them. Hope they have some good guides and they listen to their Sherpas. Everest is no place for amateurs."

"What about the Australians?" Jigger joined their conversation.

The Brit laughed. "Rodney vouched for them. Said they were all good guys and could do the mountain if they didn't let their egos blow them out before they're ready to climb it."

Jigger nodded. "Over zealous?"

"Either that or they're way more confident about their abilities than they should be," he said.

It happened to some people who had the hubris to believe that because they were athletic and quite capable with most sports, they could come to Everest and climb it without any problem or prior experience. Everest didn't take kindly to pretentious 'wannabes'. The mountain would weed out the people who didn't have the drive and mental strength to conquer it. Some would return another year and maybe even make it. Others would leave this mountain broken in some imperceptible way, never to climb again.

Jensen believed standing on the summit was his reward for knowing how insignificant he was compared to the might of Everest. The Himalayan mountain range was over sixty millions years old and had been there long before humans walked the earth. It would be there when humans died off. Jensen's moment on the mountain was a mere second in time and he would leave no mark on it.

He yawned, tired from the long hike up to camp from Lukla and the thinner air he still had to get used to. Stretching, he looked at Jigger. "I'm going to turn in early tonight."

Jigger waved at him and he thanked the Brits for their hospitality. By the time he reached the end of his expedition, he'd probably call most of the people he met at Base Camp friends.

After zipping up his coat and tugging on his hat, he turned on his flashlight then began his trudge back.

High and Rodney were still in the main tent, going over some maps when Jensen wandered past. He waved to them before entering his home for the next month or so.

Once he got out of his jacket and layers of fleece, he stripped then changed into thick sweats and a heavy sweatshirt. Jensen got settled in his sleeping bag, glad that he had gotten a new one before he left. He pulled out the notebook he'd started writing Toby letters in and opened it to the one he'd started that morning before they'd left their last stop.

After digging out his pen, he picked up where he left off, describing the scenery and how he felt reaching Base Camp. He wanted Toby to know how it felt like his journey was just now starting and how everything leading up to that moment had just been an appetizer to the main course.

* * * *

Toby jerked upright when the door to his office flew open to slam against the wall. Simpson caught it as it ricocheted back toward him. Blinking, Toby tried to figure out what time it was and why Simpson was glaring at him as though he were furious with Toby.

"What? Did I miss a deadline or something?" Toby scrambled through the papers on his desk, trying to shake the sleep out of his head.

"Have you been home in the past twenty-four hours?" Simpson stood, glaring at him with his hands propped on his hips.

Rubbing his eyes, Toby thought. "I think so. I must have, because I wasn't wearing this shirt yesterday," he muttered.

"Christ! Toby, you look like shit. Aren't you sleeping?" Simpson held up his finger to keep Toby from saying anything. "I'll be right back. Don't fall asleep."

Toby braced his elbow on the desk then rested his chin in his hand as he studied the graphs on his screen. He was pretty sure he should know what they all meant, but at that very moment, he couldn't make sense of anything except that he missed Jensen.

"God, you are pathetic," he muttered as he shoved his hand through his hair. "It's not like he died or anything. He's just on the other side of the world climbing a big fucking mountain that could kill him at any time."

"Quit fucking obsessing about it," Simpson growled at him as he stomped back into the office. This time he held a large mug that held steaming coffee — or at least Toby hoped it did. "Here. I doctored it up for you. Five sugar and a shit-ton of that god-awful French vanilla creamer you like." Simpson shuddered.

Toby took a sip then moaned as the warm liquid hit his tongue. He couldn't wait until the sugar and caffeine hit his blood stream. He watched as his friend took his usual seat. Before Simpson could start in on him, he said, "I didn't get much sleep last night. I guess I got thinking about everything that could happen to Jensen and I checked the weather and there was a storm on Everest yesterday."

"Would Jensen have been on the mountain when it hit?"

He appreciated the fact that Simpson didn't tell him not to worry about it. He'd heard enough platitudes from his parents when he talked to them throughout the week while Jensen was trekking up to Base Camp. He shrugged.

"I'm not sure. He would've made it to Base Camp at some point the day before yesterday and he'd said they were going to rest for two days to acclimatize before starting."

Simpson leaned back in the chair and frowned. "How do they do that? Aren't they already used to breathing thin air from the walk they took to get there?"

Toby chuckled. "Well, they get used to it at the different altitudes they're at, but as they get farther up the mountain, the air gets thinner and there's less oxygen. That's why Jensen thinks it'll take them between thirty-five and forty days all together to get to the summit and down again."

"Holy fuck," Simpson swore. "I guess I figured once they got there, they'd just dash up, plant a flag at the summit then race down to be back home in a couple of weeks. Almost two months to climb a freaking mountain? That's crazy."

"If they aren't careful, they can get altitude sickness."

"Which is what exactly?" Simpson shot him a look as though he were speaking a foreign language.

And in a way Toby was. He was speaking 'mountaineering' to a man who had never even known a sport like it existed until Jensen showed up again.

"It's when your body gets sick because it's not getting enough oxygen and you're dehydrating from ascending too quickly. Have you ever heard of the bends?"

Simpson nodded. "Sure. It's what divers get when they come back to the surface too fast."

"Right. Well, think of altitude sickness as the bends for mountain climbers. They ascend above six thousand five hundred feet too quickly and they can get sick. From what Jensen said, most people had recovered from it as they had grown accustomed to whatever altitude they're at. But for some, it had led to pulmonary edema or cerebral edema, which can be fatal." Toby fidgeted with his mug. "That's why it takes them two months to climb the freaking mountain."

"Okay. I get it then, but man, you have to get some sleep or you're going to end up getting sick or something. Is it worry for Jensen climbing that's doing it? Or are you back to thinking he might not return?" Simpson shook his head. "I don't mean he'll end up dead on that stupid mountain or anything drastic like that. Are you worried that he'll fall more in love with climbing than he is with you?"

Toby stared into his coffee, wishing he could see the future in the swirling light brown liquid. "It would be stupid to freak out about that. We're married, for Christ's sake. If I thought he'd ever love someone — or something — more than me, I would've never agreed to go through with it."

"Of course, it's stupid, but you know what? Emotions are rarely intelligent. You know he loves you, Toby, but it was climbing that got him sober and clean. A guy doesn't let that get away from him."

Glaring at his best friend, Toby took a deep breath. "This is bullshit. I have got to let it all go. Jensen and I are married. He'll be coming back in June. In August, we're going to have a huge party to celebrate. And for Christmas, I'm taking him to Australia to soak up the sun for two weeks before he leaves to climb another snow-covered peak."

Simpson pursed his lips as though he wanted to say something else, but Toby shook his head.

"I don't want to hear any more about Jensen not coming back, Simpson. If you really are my best friend, you'll be happy for me and support me through the next two months."

He dropped his gaze to the framed photo on his desk. It had been taken the day before Toby had flown back home in February. Cat had snapped it without them knowing about it. It was the most perfect picture of love Toby had ever seen. They were staring into each other's eyes, oblivious to whatever was going on around them. Love shone on every inch of their faces.

"It wasn't this hard when I knew he was in Wyoming," he mumbled.

A snort made him lift his head to see Simpson grinning at him. "It wasn't because you could charter a plane and be out there in a matter of hours. Now that he's in Nepal, it'll take you an entire day to get to him, if not longer."

"Thank you so much for that reminder," he quipped, sarcasm dripping from his voice.

"Always glad to help." Simpson pushed to his feet. "All right. Now that you're caffeinated and hopped up on sugar, you should be good to go for a couple hours. I'll come and get you for lunch, which you'll be buying. Then tonight I'll come out and spend the night. We can drive in together tomorrow. Maybe having someone else in the house with you will help."

Toby wanted to protest. He wasn't a child who needed reassurance from his parents or anything like that. It wasn't like he hadn't learned how to be alone while Jensen was gone, but for some reason, it just seemed harder this time. He touched his ring, vowing he'd get through this.

When Jensen returned, he'd find Toby doing fine and not having a nervous breakdown. *Only one more trip like this then Jensen won't go anywhere without you.*

"Thanks, Simpson. I'll owe you."

"Oh, you will owe me and I plan on collecting at some point." Simpson winked before he left.

Chapter Eleven

*If you cannot understand that there is something in man
which responds to the challenge of this mountain and goes
out to meet it, that the struggle is the struggle of life itself
upward and forever upward, then you won't see why we go.*

– Sir George Mallory

"All right. Everyone have crampons on?"

High checked to make sure they all had put on them
on. Jensen had 'step-in' crampons that fit to his plastic
climbing boots like ski bindings. They were going to
need them to climb up the Icefall and through most of
the way to their destination.

Once he was sure everyone was set, High said,
"We've all gone up to Camp Two and come down
again. Today, we're on our way up to Camp Three.
We'll spend a few hours up there then come down."
High met each person's gaze. "I'll let you all go at your
own speed. The guides will move among you, checking
in. If at any time you feel like you can't continue, you
flag one of us down and let us know. I don't want you

pushing it and getting sick. You can return to Base Camp and try again tomorrow."

Jensen looked over at Jigger and Cat. They'd been fretting the last several days about having to climb at the pace of the others in the group. *They're happy to hear this, I bet.* Jensen was as well, though to be honest, he'd kind of liked the slower pace early on. It helped to get him used to the air and the atmosphere. He'd discovered he needed to drink a lot of water or he would start to get headaches.

He tugged on his hat then slipped on his sunglasses. After getting his gloves on, he wiggled his shoulders to make sure his backpack was in the right place so he wouldn't end up with any sores. He was going to have aching muscles. It didn't matter how fit he'd thought he was, whenever he tried to climb a mountain, he'd had the almost immediate realization that there was no one in the world fit enough to do it and not suffer aches and pains. Unless that person was Legolas and an elf who could walk on top of the snow instead of slogging through it.

Taking a deep breath, he grimaced at the scent filling his nostrils. It wasn't the clear fragrance of untouched nature. No, the air at this spot on Everest smelled like a sewer. Unfortunately, a glacier that had been around for millions of years picked up so many smells that mingled together. It had been bad enough to gag him the first time he'd inhaled. Jensen was finally getting used to it, but still there were times when he got a jolt from it.

"Let's head out, people. Remember, slow and easy. Don't push yourself too much. There's still a lot of mountain out there." High motioned for Rodney to take off. The Australian guide and one of the Sherpas carried ladders that were to be used to cross the crevasses and fissures that hide in the Icefall.

It wasn't the first time he'd had to use ladders to navigate chasms, but the few seconds before he took his first step out on to one of the steel rungs, he said a prayer. Walking across something that looked almost like a ladder he could pick up at the hardware store had taken a lot of fearlessness on his part, especially since there were times when he couldn't see the bottom of the opening he crossed over. Jensen had taken a picture of a crevasse where the Sherpas had attached the ladders. He wasn't sure he would show Toby because he didn't want his husband worrying even more about his climbing.

One other Sherpa went with them along with Cat, Jigger and a couple of other people who'd been chomping at the bit to take off. Jensen waited until the next group with their other secondary guide walked away. He was in the last team to stride out along with High, two more Sherpas and three other climbers.

High fell in beside him as the trail they took was easy at the moment. As they climbed farther up the Khumbu Icefall, they would string out into one long line, as though they were ants working their way up the leg of a picnic table to the feast at the top.

"Why aren't you up there with your friends?" High asked, though he kept his gaze on his other clients.

The three Jensen was with were the weakest climbers among them. Baylor, a heart surgeon from Atlanta, Georgia, Evans, an accountant from someplace in France and Hubert, a lorry driver from Manchester, England. Climbing Everest was their dream, pushing them through sickness and exhaustion to do it. It was only the second week they were at Base Camp and Jensen was pretty sure the surgeon wasn't going to make it to the top. Of the three, he was placing his bet on the lorry driver. The man was built like an ox, but more than that, he seemed to take to the snow and ice of Everest as though he'd been a Sherpa in a former life and was finally coming home.

Shrugging, Jensen grabbed a hold of the accountant, helping him keep his balance before he slipped and took out the others behind them. "I'm in no hurry to get to Camp Three. I'll get there and do my three hours before coming back down. When we get to the day we're going to try for the summit, I'll be out front."

"Determined to be the first of the group to get there," High said, as though he knew exactly what Jensen was thinking.

"Not really. I kind of hope we're the first group to try that day. I'd love to see it without footprints. Pristine, like it was before the first man stood at the top of the world." He laughed. "Call me a romantic, but it would be nice to have that moment before the others get there and ruin it."

He almost fell over when High clapped him on the shoulder.

"I'll do my best to give you that chance, man. I knew you had the soul of a mountaineer." High's voice held approval. Jensen's chest puffed up in pride.

Some might've considered it silly to be proud of being called a mountaineer, but that title had been bestowed on other men that Jensen admired a great deal. Sir Edmund Hillary and Tenzing Norgay, the first men to summit Everest in nineteen-fifty-three. Sir George Mallory who died while attempting to be the first in 1924. Reinhold Messner, who became the first man to climb all fourteen eight thousand meter peaks in the world. Those four men and so many others who discovered a passion for pitting themselves against nature and sometimes coming out on top.

There was still a controversy as to whether or not Mallory had made it to the summit before he'd died. Jensen didn't care. All that mattered to him was that Mallory and his partner, Andrew Irvine, had tried. Yes, getting to the summit was an amazing feat, but sometimes the more gratifying accomplishment was simply trying.

"Thank you. That's a compliment I'll cherish," he told High. "I'm glad we chose your company to go through when we decided to do this. There's no one I'd trust more to get us to the top—or to know when to call it quits and get us down safe."

High tilted his head in acknowledgement, but didn't reply as they got to the end of one of the anchored ropes. As the different guides, climbers and Sherpas went up and down the South Col route, they'd set up the ropes to get people through the Khumbu Icefall and the different camps as they moved farther up the mountain. The ladders up the Hillary Step were in place and were maintained by the Sherpas.

He waited until High had gotten the group with him attached to the line. Jensen pulled his camera out of his pack then turned around to snap a picture of Base Camp at the bottom of the Icefall. It seemed strange that all those colorful tents could be swept away if an avalanche came down at just the right angle. After tucking his camera away, Jensen took as deep a breath as he could, hooked himself to the rope before heading off after the others.

The Khumbu Icefall was a mess of ice and snow, jagged like shark teeth. There were crevasses hidden by layers of snow no one knew about until someone took a wrong step and disappeared. Hopefully if that happened, the ropes would hold until others could get there and pull them out. Also the ropes were there to keep climbers on the safest path the Sherpas and guides had found while traversing the South Col.

It was a beautiful sunny day, though the wind bit as it nipped around the edges of Jensen's jacket and hat. He was glad for his sunglasses, because the light reflecting off the white ice could've blinded him within minutes. Snow blindness was a real problem on the side of the mountain if he wasn't properly attired. He unzipped his coat, hoping not to overheat. The farther up Everest they went, the closer to the sun they got and the atmosphere thinned enough that solar radiation could become an issue as well, which was why he did his best to stay covered. Well, radiation and frostbite. No matter how warm he grew from struggling through the snow and ice, he could still die of exposure within minutes if he wasn't careful.

Little pieces of snow and ice carried by the wind struck his exposed skin, almost as though Everest chose to attack those who thought to climb her. He'd even had small cuts from where they'd hit him by the time he'd reached his tent for the night. There were sudden strong gusts that threatened to steal his breath or to freeze his lungs with the bitter chill they carried. Jensen trudged along, trying not to be captivated by the dancing eddies blown here and there by the wind. The spirits were alive and well on the ice, tempting the climbers to follow them where they lead.

As he moved along steadily but cautiously, he spotted Rodney's team in the lead farther up the Icefall. They would slow down once they got to the ladders crossing the different crevasses.

"Looks like the Brits are heading out as well," High called back to Jensen.

Jensen checked over his shoulder to see the A team for the British expedition had reached the crampon point and was attaching them while their B team was making their way from Base Camp.

"There's going to be a line up at some of these ladders," he told High, knowing that the best climbers the Brits had would soon overtake them.

"Yeah. It's all right. As long as everyone takes their turn and no one rushes, we'll all get to the same place without losing anyone." High went back to talking softly to Evans.

There was something going on with the man, but Jensen wasn't close enough to hear or see. He just hoped High either got it figured out or sent him back down to Base Camp. Taking out his camera, Jensen began to snap some more photos of all the different forms and shapes the ice took around him.

"I've never seen anything like this," Hubert, the lorry driver, said from just in front of Jensen.

They'd never climbed together during the days while going up and down from camp to camp, so Jensen had never gotten a chance to really talk to him.

"It's breathtaking, isn't it?"

Hubert turned to glance at him and Jensen took a picture. "I'd like a copy of that when we all get back to our homes."

"Of course. I have a Flickr account where I'll post all the pictures I take here. Before we split up, I'll get your email address and send you a link. You can let me know which ones you want and I'll send you the high res files for them." Jensen grinned.

"Right. I have no idea what you said." Hubert chuckled. "My son's the electronics guy in the family. He'll get me set up."

"What brings you out here? If you don't mind me saying this, Everest is a long way from Manchester and being a lorry driver." Jensen hoped Hubert wasn't offended by his question.

Hubert laughed again. "Aye, it is, but ever since my dad told me the story of Hillary's conquering Everest, I always was intrigued by the mountain and the men who dared to climb it. I swore that one day I was going to try."

"Try? Didn't you dream of standing at the summit?"

"Not really. I guess I don't dream big dreams. My wish was to travel to Nepal and come to Base Camp. I think I was pretty sure that by the time I got here, I wasn't going to be in any shape to even think about climbing Everest." Hubert swept his hand in a wide gesture, encompassing everything around them. "All the rest of this is icing on my cake and getting to the summit will be the biggest present I've ever gotten—aside from my wife and kids."

Jensen couldn't help himself. He took another picture of Hubert, wanting to capture the expression of utter joy on the man's face as he looked out over the white peaks and valleys around them.

While Hubert had said he didn't dream big dreams, Jensen wasn't sure that was right. Hubert's dream was just the right size for him. At the time he came up with it, the edges seemed to end at the base of the mountain. Yet like all dreams, Hubert's had grown until it covered everything to the very summit.

That was the nature of a dream. It started out small then each tiny step taken toward fulfillment caused the dream to expand a little farther and a little farther until it included mountains—until it contained all the love, hope, joy and promise a person could wish for.

Loving Toby had been Jensen's Everest dream. He'd done everything in his power to obtain it. Yet now that he had, the dream had morphed into something bigger than before. Like Hubert's, Jensen's had become more than a simple dream. It had become the greatest gift he could ever hope to receive.

* * * *

"Jensen's fine, Mom." Toby smiled as he spoke to his mom over the phone. "I heard from him yesterday. They'd gotten back from Camp Three and were going to take a rest day today before going back up there for a night."

"How did he sound? He's not exhausting himself, is he?"

"He sounded tired, but he'd just finished up a pretty strenuous climb." He assumed it was exhausting, no matter how cautious Jensen was. The thin air and the effort of carrying a thirty-pound backpack while trying to watch every step, had to wear out even the strongest of men.

"I bet he isn't sleeping well either, and there was another storm up there."

Closing his eyes, Toby pinched the bridge of his nose. After he'd confessed to Simpson that he was checking the weather reports for Everest every few minutes, his friend had forbidden him to do it. He had no idea how many storms they might have had since then. He didn't need his mom telling him about it, because it would only add to his own worries.

"Well, Mom, it's cold and windy up there. No matter how warm his sleeping bag is, I'm pretty sure it's not that comfortable, even at Base Camp." He wandered over to the French doors leading into the backyard.

A soft April shower had begun when Mom had called and Toby wanted to go sit under the large maple tree and listen to the drops on the leaves. But he couldn't hang up on her, not when she was babbling about weather and Jensen and too much snow.

Finally Dad took the phone. "I'm sorry, Toby. I've told her to stop checking the weather and the news reports. They're only going to give her an ulcer. How are you doing?"

He chuckled. "I'm fine, Dad. Simpson made me promise not to check any of that stuff too. He said if something happened, someone would call me and there wasn't any point in getting worked up over stuff I can't do anything about."

"I always thought Simpson was a smart man. I know your mother wanted to ask you, but she got distracted. Are you going to visit this weekend?" He cleared his throat. "You know how she loves having all her children home for Easter."

At some point in their family line, a Jewish ancestor must have converted or something, because while their last name might have been Schwartzel, they didn't practice Judaism. They were Methodists.

"Yes. I plan on heading up after work on Thursday. Abramson closed the office for Good Friday." He rested his head against the cool windowpane. "It'll be nice to see all of you," he admitted.

With Jensen gone, Toby was beginning to see how much he enjoyed having family and friends around. Simpson and several of Toby's friends had started to come out for dinner and cards on Friday nights. It was a tradition he was going to keep when Jensen returned. His other friends all liked Jensen and he was sure—with time—Simpson would as well.

"Your sisters are excited to have you visiting. They all want to discuss the wedding and reception with you." Dad sounds confused. "I'm not sure what anything they've talked to your mother is, but I've warned you."

"Thanks. I wish Jensen were here so that he could bear the brunt of their questioning on this." He sighed. "Oh well. I guess that's what I get for having a family that loves me."

"Honey," his mom took over the conversation again. "Shouldn't we try getting in touch with Jensen's parents? I know how I'd feel if I missed your wedding."

Toby gritted his teeth for a moment before saying, "No, Mom. Remember? We've talked about this like a million times. Jensen doesn't want any contact with his parents. We're not going against his wishes."

She huffed. "I just feel so bad that they don't know what a wonderful son they have."

"And apparently it was their choice. It wasn't like he'd changed his last name or something before we got married. He even went to Harvard like his dad wanted him to. At any time they could've reached out to him, but they chose not to. Besides, Mom, we are his family now. He sees you and Dad as his parents. Kelly and Wendy are his sisters." Toby's eyes filled with tears. "I think we got the better end of the deal when he agreed to become a part of our family."

"So true, honey." Mom sniffed. "All right. Well, I'll let you go. I'm sure you need to eat something then head to bed. You work too much."

He accepted her usual admonishment to eat and not work too hard then told her he loved her. After ending the call, he put his phone in his pocket, slipped on a zippered sweater before walking outside.

Toby sat on the wooden bench Jensen had built and placed under the huge maple tree. He'd done it as a surprise for Toby after he'd mentioned that the tree was one of the reasons why he bought the place. Toby had imagined them sitting under it at twilight, watching fireflies dance through the grass and flowers.

The night Jensen had revealed the bench, they'd done just as Toby had envisioned and it had been perfect.

Chapter Twelve

We will stomp to the top with the wind in our teeth.

– Sir George Mallory

Jensen tried not to grip his ice pick too hard as he stared at the openings between the rungs of the ladder he was walking on. *Why did I ever think climbing this stupid mountain would be fun? I mean really? What possessed me to say yes?*

"Just one more rung, Schwartzel," High told him. He did what he'd done for the others crossing the crevasse. He'd encouraged them every step of the way, even Evans, who'd frozen halfway across and had to be forced to finish the rest of the distance.

He didn't know what had made it different this time for Evans. They'd taken those ladders up and down for the last two weeks on their way up to the other camps. Hell, they'd even gotten all the way up to Camp Three. None of those trips had been an issue for the Frenchman, yet there had been something bothering him all day and Jensen didn't know if he was going to be able to complete the climb.

Jensen couldn't worry about someone else at the moment. He still needed to take one more step then he'd be off the ladder and they could move on to Camp Three at the base of Lhotse Face. They'd spend the night before heading back down to Camp Two in the morning. They'd spend the night there then head down to Base Camp.

High had one more climb up to Camp Three planned then they would make the summit bid. The weather had been rough the last couple of days, with high winds and snow falling in unpredictable patterns. Nothing Jensen couldn't deal with, but for some reason, that day he'd been having trouble with the heat as they climbed through the Western Cwm.

Once he got off the ladder, he crouched to the side, letting the others head on without him for a moment. He took one breath, filling his lungs as best he could then exhaling before inhaling again.

"Solar radiation is a bitch," Rodney said from where he stood, waiting for Jensen.

"Yeah." Jensen straightened. "All right. Let's go."

"Good on ya', mate." Rodney hooked his jamar to the rope and started to ratchet himself up along the fixed line.

Closing his eyes, Jensen cleared his fogged mind as best he could before following Rodney up. Once getting into Camp Three, he took a bottle of Gatorade from one of the Sherpas who'd come up before them. After thanking him, Jensen drank down the entire thing.

Jigger and Cat had been in camp at least an hour, having started out earlier than Jensen. They were melting water for them to drink. All of the tents for his expedition were pitched on platforms the Sherpas had carved out of the ice on the side of the mountain, and the Brits who were coming up behind them were settled a little higher up.

"We have some water for you to drink," Cat called to Jensen, who ended up not being the last one in.

High had stayed with Evans and Baylor, both of whom were struggling that day. Rodney had trudged in with Jensen then went back down to help High when a radio call had come in.

"Is everything all right with Evans and Baylor?" Jensen asked Hubert, who'd trailed in a few minutes after Rodney had left.

"I'm not sure. I passed them about halfway down and High seemed to be really talking to Evans. Couldn't hear what he was saying. Baylor just sat on a block of ice and didn't seem interested in moving either." Hubert rubbed his hand over his face and sighed.

"Go get in your tent and warm up. I'll bring you some water." Jensen was starting to feel better. His head cleared and it was a little easier to breathe.

Coleman, the expedition's third guide, emerged from his tent and stared down the mountain. Jensen wandered over to him, knowing he should be getting in his sleeping bag and drinking, but he had to know what was going on.

"Have you heard from High?"

Shooting him a quick glance, Coleman nodded. "High's taking Evans and Baylor back down to Base Camp. He'll spend the night down there and come back up here tomorrow to help us get down to Camp Two."

"Maybe he should just stay at Base Camp and meet us at Camp One. I think, as long as Rodney's up here with you, the rest of us will be okay," Jensen suggested. "He has the two least experienced climbers with him."

"You're right, but I don't think he'll risk leaving us all up here on our own. Rodney's got a lot of time on Everest, but I don't. I've only done the climb once and I didn't even summit that time." Coleman rubbed the back of his head. "I'll radio him and see what he has to say."

"Did he say what's wrong with them?"

Coleman shook his head. "No. You can ask Rodney. He should be back here in about twenty minutes."

It was a good thing, because the sun would be setting soon and no one wanted to be climbing in the dark. Most would be in their tents, trying to stay warm as the wind howled around them. Rodney had become Jensen's tent mate over the course of the climb, so he knew he could catch up on the news when Rodney returned.

He checked in with Cat and Jigger, both of whom looked whipped. He made sure they had water, Gatorade and food. "I'm leaving for Camp Two at around four in the morning."

"We'll probably wait until six," Jigger told him, his voice hoarse. He'd been complaining about a sore throat and difficulty breathing the day before. Jensen thought his friend needed to slow down a little. Jigger had been pushing himself a lot harder than Jensen had.

"Cool. I'm going to climb in my tent. I'll see you at Camp Two tomorrow." He gave Cat a hug before leaving.

After settling in his sleeping bag, Jensen tugged out a notebook and pen he'd tucked in his backpack. He knew he wouldn't be writing anything when they did their push to the summit since they weren't stopping anywhere on the way down. Just going to the summit and back to Base Camp. There would be a short stop at

Camp Four to pick up another supplemental oxygen tank on the way down.

It was the second notebook he'd used during the trip. The first one was full of his thoughts and observations of the people and scenery around him. He knew Toby would love reading about the day-to-day routines of climbing a mountain. It was going to be a fun way, along with all the pictures he'd taken, to look back on the adventure.

He'd called Toby the last time they were at Base Camp, but he'd told him that he wouldn't be calling until after the summit try. He needed to keep his mind focused entirely on the climb. Getting distracted with thoughts of Toby could cause him to make a mistake and that was the one thing he didn't want to do at twenty-six thousand feet.

Jensen had just finished up his letter and was getting ready to put the notebook away for the night when Rodney unzipped the flap before almost falling in. Jensen caught the guide before he landed on his face. He helped Rodney get out of his jacket while making sure he had water.

Once Rodney was tucked into his sleeping bag, a Sherpa delivered a bowl of Ramen noodles and more water for him. Jensen took it then fed it to him because Rodney's hands were trembling from the cold. When the bowl was empty, he stuck it in the corner of the tent, making a note to find a Sherpa in the morning and return it.

"Holy fuck, man. It's cold out there. Not sure if a storm's moving in or something, but I told everyone to stay in their tents tonight." Rodney covered his blond hair with a wool hat then put gloves on. "What time were you thinking of heading out?"

"At four."

Rodney nodded. "High said you'd start heading out before the others, now that we're so close to the push."

Jensen shrugged. "I was conserving what energy I could. There aren't any prizes for being the first into each of the camps. The important thing is the summit, plus I think my plodding along has helped me acclimatize a little better. Still not going without oxygen to the top."

He grinned and Rodney snorted.

"A couple of the Brits are going to try it," Rodney told him.

"Good luck to them. I just hope they have a guide that'll stay close because from what I understand, it's the coming down that gets a little hairy when you don't have oxygen to breathe." He shifted in his sleeping bag. "What happened to Evans and Baylor?"

"Not sure. Evans doesn't seem to be sick, played out or anything like that. I think he's scared. Everest is more than he thought it would be. Some people are arrogant that way. They see a picture of it and they say, 'it's just a mountain'. All they see is the rock and the snow. Some people don't see that Everest is so much more. It's a dream and a goal."

"It's a killer if you don't respect it," Jensen pointed out.

Rodney nodded. "Aye. Without respect, it will crush a person and that's what happened to Evans, I think. His ego was bigger than his ability."

He'd seen other people in some of the other expeditions who could be described that way as well. Jensen wondered how many of them would make it.

"What about Baylor? He didn't strike me as that kind of person." Jensen lay down, shoving and tweaking his pack that he used as a pillow. He tried not to think about the perfect pillow he had on his bed at home.

Rodney wiggled and grunted while he got arranged in his own sleeping bag. "He's sick. Not sure what's wrong, but it's not his courage that's the problem. High didn't know either. Figured they'd get him checked out by the doctors at Base Camp."

"I hope it's nothing major," Jensen murmured. As much he hadn't been fond of either man, he didn't want them to get hurt.

"He stopped right after the ladder you got over. I saw him there, but High was with him and Evans, so I stayed with you and the others around you. I'm going to send Coleman down with the little group going with you. I'll come down later with the others." Rodney coughed then sighed. "I'm not going to get much sleep tonight."

Jensen agreed. "Maybe when we get back to one of the lower camps, the wind won't be so bad."

Rodney didn't answer and he figured it was simply because the guide didn't want to waste any more air — and energy — than he needed. Jensen rolled over onto his back, staring up at the ceiling of the tent. He listened to the nylon flutter as the wind howled by. It sounded as though there were monsters battling outside their enclosure. He wondered if he looked outside, would there be yetis fighting?

He'd spent so many nights trying to sleep, only to have the very air around him do its hardest to keep him awake. Everest fought the people who tried to climb her, reluctantly giving up an inch, but claiming a piece of a climber's spirit with every step he took. Jensen knew that while he'd be able to say he summitted Everest and be proud of it, only other people who were on the mountain with him, would understand the toll it took on his deepest soul.

You're getting too fanciful. It's just a mountain. Nothing more or less than what it seems. Shaking his head, he closed his eyes to try and see if he'd be able to get any kind of sleep. Probably not at the higher camps. When they got back down to Base Camp, it wouldn't be so bad. Maybe he wouldn't be so exhausted and while he lay in the darkness, listening to the power of nature whipping by him, he could admit to himself that he was exhausted. Not taking the lead to break the trail or even just trying to get into the camps first hadn't really saved him any energy, though he thought he was a little better off than Jigger and Cat.

"When we start the push, it's going to be worse," Rodney whispered.

Jensen didn't acknowledge what Rodney said, though he knew it would be. He had a feeling he wouldn't be getting any sleep until he came down the mountain for the last time. *Why do I love climbing mountains? Why lose billions of brain cells to spend five minutes at the top?* He could almost hear Toby asking him those questions.

He pondered them and he couldn't come up with a good answer — because he could do it while not everyone else could, because it was a better high than he'd gotten from any drug or alcohol. It was proving he had the courage to do something most of the population wouldn't.

"Because I'm hoping my parents will see my name on the news and will be proud to say I'm their child," he murmured into the wind-battered silence of the tent.

Either Rodney chose to ignore him or the guide had passed out in exhaustion. Jensen was glad, since he hadn't wanted to admit what he'd just said to anyone. Yet while he thought that, he found himself wishing that Toby were there, if only to hold him tightly and tell him that he was proud of Jensen, that Jensen didn't need his parents because Toby loved him and would be more than happy to proclaim it to the world.

Hell, he didn't need to climb a freaking mountain to get Toby to do that.

* * * *

"I fucking miss him, Simpson," Toby slurred as Simpson slung his arm around his shoulders then started moving him upstairs.

"I know you do, but remember…if you love something, you set it free. If it comes back to you, it's yours. If it doesn't, then it's fucking stupid," Simpson said.

Toby squinted as he tried to get his alcohol-soaked brain to process what his friend had said. "I don't think that was the actual saying."

"I don't really care what the saying was, Toby. No more liquor for you. You're not supposed to have any in the house anyway." Simpson snorted. "Jensen's going to be disappointed in you."

"Why? I never took the oath of sobriety. I did it because it was easier not to when he was here." Toby exhaled loudly when Simpson dropped him on his bed.

Simpson tugged off Toby's shoes and his belt, but left him dressed. "I'm going to leave some aspirin and a bottle of water on the night stand. This will *not* happen again. No more drinking while he's away. Hell, it's not like you don't know where he is, plus he'll be home soon. You can man up and be strong for that long, can't you?"

Toby burped and Simpson rolled his eyes.

"I'm pathetic, aren't I?" he asked his friend.

"Yes, but you're in love and your husband is halfway around the world from you, doing something extremely stupid and reckless." Simpson patted his shoulder. "You have the right to be pathetic, but only once. From now on, you'll suck it up and hold yourself together, so that when he gets back, you're aren't going to need therapy or a hospital."

He grabbed a hold of Simpson's hand before he walked off. When Simpson turned to look at him, he tried to smile. Toby wasn't sure how well it turned out since he couldn't really feel his face. "Thank you. You've been a really good friend to me for all these years."

"Only giving back to you, Toby. You've taken care of me when I needed you as well. Get some sleep. I'll call you in the morning to make sure you're okay."

Toby rolled onto his stomach, burying his face in Jensen's pillow. He flapped his hand in Simpson's direction to let him know he'd heard him. He listened as Simpson walked down the hall to the stairs. That was the last thing he remembered.

Chapter Thirteen

*While on top of Everest, I looked across the valley towards
the great peak Makalu and mentally worked out a route of
how it could be climbed. It showed me that even though I
was standing at the top of the world, it wasn't the end of
everything. I was still looking beyond to other interesting
challenges.*

– Sir Edmund Hillary

It hadn't even reached midnight when Jensen headed
out of Camp Four, continuing on the summit push.
He'd spent his time in the tent, breathing in bottled
oxygen and had a restless night, not really liking the
feel of the mask on his face. It had been the second night
in a row that he hadn't slept. The weather forecast had
called for fairly good weather, but of course, on Everest,
no one could plan anything.

Jigger and Cat had already left, but Jensen knew he'd
probably catch up to them along the way. Rodney
joined him and nodded. Before they got started, he
gestured to the darkness above them.

"Two of the Brits and one of their guides already went on as well," Rodney informed him.

A hint of disappointment hit Jensen. He probably wasn't going to be the first at the summit that day. Then he shook his head. It didn't matter who got there first, as long as he made it. All the time away from Toby would be worth it once he put a foot at the top of the world.

"Ready?" Rodney grinned at him before putting his oxygen mask on.

Jensen made sure his regulator was working then nodded. It was time to leave the South Col and drag his exhausted ass upward into the Death Zone, the area above twenty-seven thousand feet. He'd put his two canisters of oxygen in his pack, using one and having one for back up. He'd grab another one at the South Summit.

Two of the sirdars, head Sherpas, for the Brits and for High's group, had gone out a few hours before the climbers were to leave to blaze a trail and lay the fixed ropes up to the summit. Since they were to be the first teams to try, they needed the ropes set.

By the time Jensen and Rodney had worked their way around some of the slower climbers, the Sherpas headed down to greet them. Jigger and Cat were still ahead of them somewhere in the darkness, but he'd gotten ahead of the Brits.

"What's it like up there," Rodney called out.

"Snow is deep, but weather good so far. Ropes are solid," High's sirdar told them.

"Thanks."

They waved as they continued on, probably to help others who might need it as they moved toward the summit. Jensen plodded along, doing his best to keep his mind focused on where he put his feet and his ice pick. At this altitude, it was dangerous to let his thoughts wander from his purpose, which was to climb the freaking mountain.

It wasn't long before he caught up with Jigger and Cat, who seemed to have slowed down some. He patted Cat on the back, recognizing her bright blue climbing suit. She stopped and he unclipped his rope to go around her. He did the same thing as he reached Jigger. His friend grinned at him, giving him a thumbs up.

Jensen had been following Rodney, but suddenly the guide stopped. Rodney looked over his shoulder at him then with a smile, he motioned Jensen forward. After taking three of the most exhausting steps of his life, Jensen was there. He stood at the top of the world. At that moment, no one was higher than him, unless they were in an airplane.

The summit was clear and he glanced around at all the other peaks in the Himalayan range. He saw Annapurna I – the one some considered the deadliest of the eight thousand meter mountains. For every two people who summitted it, one died. Jensen had never considered climbing that one. The risk was too high. Makalu was visible as well, while the rest were wreathed with clouds.

He put one of his feet on the Chinese side of Everest, just for a second to be able to say he was there. After tugging out his camera, he snapped a quick picture of the scenery. Rodney tapped him on the shoulder, gesturing toward the camera. Nodding, Jensen pulled a piece of paper out of his pocket while Rodney got it ready. He held it up and Rodney snapped the photo.

Jensen took one of Rodney striking a summit pose then he stuffed it away before he started back down the mountain. It was time to get the hell out of Dodge and down to Base camp. Now that he had reached his goal, Jensen was ready to go home. Plus he was getting low on oxygen. It was time to get down to the South Summit and pick up his third oxygen canister.

He wanted to get to back to Camp Four and crash for a while. Hopefully by the time he'd gotten some rest, the others would be done. As he went past Jigger and Cat, who were still working their way up, he waved then struggled on. He crouched out of the way at the top of the Hillary Step while a line of climbers moved along the ropes. Jensen figured he was running low on oxygen, but he still had enough to get him where he could resupply.

Coleman was the last one up the rope and he stopped to grin at Jensen. "Congratulations, man. The Step is clear, so you can keep going. High's bringing up the rear with Hubert and the rest."

They had a definite turnaround time of two o'clock and when Jensen checked his watch, he saw there was still a good hour and half left. He hoped the others were climbing at a fast enough pace to get them up to the top.

"Thanks. Go on up. It was clear and sunny when I left," Jensen told Coleman before clipping on to the line that would keep him safe — or as safe as he could be this high on Everest.

Working his way down, Jensen wiggled his fingers, not liking how he was losing sensation in them. Yet he still had a long time to get to his tent and some tea from the Sherpas High had ordered to stay behind.

After getting through the Step without incident, Jensen ran into High and the others a few yards away from the base. Hubert and the others seemed to be moving well, if a little slower than the rest. Jensen really hoped that Hubert would be able to realize a far bigger dream than he'd ever planned on.

"How are you doing?" High asked, yelling over the suddenly blowing wind.

"Struggling a little, but I'll be okay. The rest are still going strong. Left Rodney at the summit. Assume he was waiting for Jigger and Cat, who were right behind us." Each word was a struggle to get out.

"Good. I'll see them farther up the mountain then." High grinned at him. "You did it, Schwartzel. You climbed Everest."

"Yeah." Jensen patted Hubert's arm before going around them.

Elation hit him when he got to the stash of extra oxygen and got a new one hooked up to his regulator before he stumbled away toward the Balcony. Taking his time, Jensen got to Camp Four just fine. He fell into his tent with a deep sigh, accepting the tea one of the Sherpas had boiled for the climbers. They gave him several cups and he slowly began to warm up a little. Hell, he figured he wasn't going to get back to his normal body temperature for several weeks after he got home.

Snuggling in his sleeping bag, he dug out his notebook and wrote a quick note to Toby before his eyes drifted shut. Maybe he should be worried about the others as the wind began to blow even harder, but Jensen couldn't bring himself to fret at the moment. All he could think about was closing his eyes and trying to regain some of the energy he'd used up during the push to the top.

* * * *

Jensen staggered off the plane. His head pounded from jet lag, lack of sleep and, of course, oxygen deprivation. He hadn't given his body enough time to recover before he flew home.

He'd done his part, making sure Cat and Jigger made it back to Wyoming without issue, then caught the first flight he could to La Guardia. All Jensen wanted to do was wrap Toby in his arms for an hour—or until Toby made him let go. Then he wanted to burrow under the blankets of their bed and sleep for a day or two. After that, he might begin to feel human again.

When he got to the right baggage claim carousel, he glanced around to see if he could spot Toby.

"You look like hammered shit, man."

Jensen jumped when Simpson spoke from right behind him. Whirling, he glared at the man and hated the fact Simpson had to grab his arm to keep him from falling over.

"That's what happens when you climb Mount fucking Everest, jackass. Where's Toby?"

He wasn't in the mood to deal with Simpson, who had never made any bones about how he was pretty sure Jensen would just forget to come home after one of his trips. So far Toby hadn't believed him and Jensen loved him even more for that. Though he had the feeling that one more time might be the straw that broke the camel's back.

"He's been working himself to death since you flew out to Wyoming five months ago. I'm not sure he's been home for more than a few days at a time." Simpson frowned at him.

"Well, let's grab my bag and go get him out of there. Once home, he and I can curl up in bed for a couple of days and just sleep. Simpson, I know you care about Toby and I really appreciate all the shit you do for him when I'm gone, but I can't deal with you right now. I can't even think straight." Jensen closed his eyes and took a deep breath.

Simpson encircled his waist, holding him close. "All right, man. You need to get home then I'm sure Toby's going to take you to a doctor. He's going to want to make sure you're okay."

Jensen didn't really care what happened later. All he wanted was Toby and his bed. "Whatever."

He lost track of time as they stood waiting for the bags to come. When his appeared, he pointed at it.

"That's mine."

"You only packed one bag? Doesn't seem like nearly enough shit to be gone for five months." Simpson frowned as he yanked the duffle off the belt.

"Cat's shipping the rest back to me sometime next week. I didn't want to pay for extra luggage plus I didn't want to take more time getting back here." Jensen shuffled in the direction of the exit. "How far away is your car?"

Simpson laughed. "We don't need to discuss that. Just keep close and try not to wander off. I don't want to tell Toby I lost you in the airport because you were too tired to see straight."

"You might want to tie me to you. I'm not entirely sure I'll be able to walk straight for much longer." He was only half joking.

"I need one of those leashes you see parents put on their kids," Simpson muttered as he took Jensen's elbow with his hand to direct him through the crowds out to the parking garages.

At some point, Jensen checked out, trusting Simpson to get him to the car. It wasn't until he woke up with Simpson shaking his shoulder that he realized they had left the airport and driven through the city to the building where Toby worked.

"While I go get you some coffee and something to eat, you can run up and get Toby from his office. They won't have a problem with him leaving early. Hell, with as much overtime as he's worked the last couple of months, he could take a week or two off without any difficulty."

Rubbing his dry eyes, Jensen grunted his agreement as he climbed out of the car. He strolled into the building and nodded at the security guard sitting at the desk.

"Hey Thomas, how are you doing?"

Thomas grinned. "Jensen. It's good to see you, dude. Toby said you were going to be home soon."

"Just got in. Going to remove Toby from his office and take him home." Jensen managed to wink at Thomas as he walked past to the elevators.

"Great. He's looking a lot like you are. Definitely get some rest. Both of you."

Jensen waved as he stepped into the elevator then punched the button for Toby's floor. He propped himself up against the wall, letting his eyes drift shut for the ride up. When it dinged, he checked to see if it was the right one, but it stopped two floors below Toby's.

He didn't pay any attention to who got on with him until he heard a gasp and he shot up.

"You're here."

Toby stood staring at him and Jensen didn't think. After reaching out, he grabbed him then jerked him into his arms. Toby dropped the papers he was carrying before embracing him. Their mouths smashed together and Jensen tasted a hint of blood, but he didn't care about his cracked lips. All he cared about was relearning everything about the man he loved.

He'd forgotten where they were until the sound of someone clearing their throat caused him to break their kiss. Looking up over Toby's head, he saw Abramson, Toby's supervisor, standing there, holding the elevator doors open.

"Toby, I think you should take the rest of the day off," Abramson said.

Jensen chuckled when Toby hid his face in his shoulder. "He's going to take you up on that suggestion."

Abramson smiled. "Glad you made it home, Brockhoff. Congratulations."

"It's Schwartzel now. I changed my last name when we got married," he explained when Abramson frowned.

"Ah. Right. I had forgotten that. Well, pick up those papers and leave them on Benson's desk. He can take care of them. Why don't you take the rest of the week off? I'm pretty sure you'll be worthless for a little while." Abramson winked before walking away.

Jensen let go of Toby then crouched, moaning at the ache in his knees. "Come on, honey. Get a move on. We don't want him to change his mind."

Toby didn't say anything and Jensen glanced up to see Toby staring down at him with tears in his eyes. He surged up to wrap his arms around him again.

"What's wrong? Are you okay? I didn't hurt you, did I?" He leaned back a little to look at Toby.

Shaking his head, Toby inhaled sharply then said, "No. I'm just so happy that you're home."

"So am I," he whispered. "But let's go to our house so I can hold your naked body to mine and remember what it's like to be warm."

Toby nodded. Together, they gathered the papers then dropped them off with Benson. Toby grabbed his jacket and his messenger bag before Jensen took his hand and they rode the elevator down to the ground level. With a wave to Thomas, Jensen dragged Toby to where Simpson was still parked at the curb.

He got the back door open for Toby to slide in. After joining him, he tapped Simpson on the back of the head. "Take us home, James."

"Shut up, asshole," Simpson said, but put the car in drive before pulling into traffic.

Jensen pulled Toby into his side, resting his head on top of Toby's. He breathed in the familiar spicy scent of his lover and sighed. He was home. It didn't matter that he wasn't in their house. Toby was his home—the rest was just sticks and nails.

P a r t   T w o

K 2

"…just the bare bones of a name, all rock and ice and storm and abyss. It makes no attempt to sound human. It is atoms and stars. It has the nakedness of the world before the first man — or of the cindered planet after the last."

— Fosco Maraini

Chapter Fourteen

*Being deeply loved by someone gives you strength, while
loving someone deeply gives you courage.*

— Lao Tzu

Toby leaned on his elbow to stare down at Jensen,
who was curled up as though he was still trying to get
warm. The first week that Jensen had been home from
Everest, he'd clung to Toby during the night, holding
on to him as if he thought Toby was going to disappear.
He ran his finger along the ridge of Jensen's nose then
rubbed his thumb over Jensen's bottom lip.

It had taken that entire week for Jensen's skin to heal
from the dehydration and windburn he'd suffered
while on the mountain. He was also finally putting
back on the thirty-five pounds he'd lost.

Glancing over at the clock, Toby grinned. They still
had time before they needed to get up and pack the car
to head to his parents. This weekend was their second
wedding and reception—both of which would take

place in his parents' backyard. His dad had insisted on it and Toby saw no reason to argue with him.

But that was for later. Right now, he had the perfect way to wake his husband up. Toby nudged Jensen softly to encourage him to lie on his back. When Jensen mumbled but didn't seem to wake, Toby got him situated with his legs spread wide so Toby could settle between them.

Jensen's cock slowly hardened as Toby teased and played with it. He licked along the underside before pressing the tip of his tongue to the slit. Pinning Jensen's hips to the mattress, Toby got started with the blow job.

"Toby," Jensen murmured, as he reached down to smooth his hand over Toby's hair.

His mouth full, Toby couldn't speak but he hummed and Jensen shuddered as the vibration surrounded his flesh. Toby bobbed his head up and down, applying as much suction as he could and drawing a low moan from Jensen.

Pre-cum coated his mouth as Toby swallowed down the thick column. He scrambled for the bottle of lube he'd grabbed from the bathroom when he woke earlier. After getting his fingers slick, Toby slipped them down behind Jensen's balls to rub over his taint then to the puckered opening. Jensen wiggled and shifted, trying to get Toby to touch him harder.

"Toby, more," Jensen begged.

He was happy to oblige. Letting Jensen ease out of his mouth until just his head was there, Toby worked it then pressed two of his fingers in.

"Oh!" Jensen tried to arch his hips but Toby kept him still.

"Does it hurt?" He asked, not wanting to cause Jensen any pain, but wanting to get him stretched fast.

Jensen shook his head. "No. I want more."

Eyebrows raised, Toby looked up to see Jensen staring down at him. When their gazes met, Jensen winked.

"I won't break, Toby. Get some more lube in there then fuck me. It might seem weird since I've been home for a month already, but I'm still feeling empty after being away for so long." Jensen licked his lips. "I need you inside me."

There was no way he was going to ignore that. Toby rushed to get more lube into Jensen's channel. Even though he rushed a little, he did do his best to get Jensen to relax enough that it wouldn't hurt too badly when he pushed in.

He grunted when Jensen pinched his side. "What?"

"Now." Jensen glared at him and Toby grinned.

"All right. You're being very demanding this morning," Toby commented while coating his cock then positioned at Jensen's hole.

"I dreamt I was stuck on the Balcony of Everest and it was snowing so hard, I couldn't see how to get down. All I could think about was how you were going to hate me because I didn't come back this time," Jensen admitted.

Toby touched Jensen's cheek. "Oh honey, why didn't you say something? I didn't know you were having nightmares like that. Have you been having them often?"

Jensen shook his head. "I don't want to talk about it right now. I want you to make love to me. I want to come on your cock."

Inhaling sharply, Toby nodded. They'd discuss Jensen's dreams later. It was time for him to reassure his lover that he wasn't going to leave him either. Pressing in, he eased slowly inch by inch, studying

Jensen's face for the slightest hint that Jensen was in pain. There was nothing but love and need shining in those hazel eyes Toby loved so much.

When he was buried all the way in, Toby stilled and sighed. He adored how perfectly they fit together, whether he was topping or bottoming. All that mattered was how close making love brought them. He could ignore everything else going on in the world.

Curling up, Jensen kissed him fiercely then lay back on the sheets. "Move," he ordered Toby.

"All right."

He gripped Jensen's hips as he began to thrust in and out, slow and easy as first. Jensen clenched his inner passage to draw a moan from Toby. He tilted Jensen's hips a little more and stroked in. When Jensen jerked, Toby chuckled.

"Right there," he muttered then proceeded to hit Jensen's gland every time he slid.

As Jensen moved in counter rhythm to him, Toby began to speed up, eventually slamming into him as fast and as hard as he could. Jensen pressed one hand against the headboard to keep from hitting his head and wrapped his other hand around his cock then pumped.

"Oh Christ! Again, Toby. Harder."

Jensen let his head fall back and Toby leaned forward to lick a line from the base of his throat up to his mouth where they dueled for control of the kiss while Toby continued to ride Jensen. He knew Jensen would probably be sporting bruises by the end of the day, but he knew Jensen wouldn't care about it.

Like Toby always loved how his ass ached after Jensen took him, Jensen always seemed to like the bruises Toby often left on his skin. At least Toby thought he did since he'd caught Jensen touching them when he thought Toby hadn't been looking.

The familiar pressure built in Toby's groin and his smooth movements became rough. Suddenly, Jensen came and his body tightened around Toby's cock like a vise. It was as though he was trying to milk every last drop of cum from Toby, which worked because Toby climaxed seconds later. He flooded Jensen as they both trembled and panted while the waves of pleasure rippled through them.

Toby carefully slid his softened length out of Jensen then reached for a towel he'd left on the floor after his shower the night before. After cleaning both of them, he tossed the towel in the direction of the bathroom. Once he was done, he embraced Jensen, pulling him close enough for Jensen to rest his head on his chest.

"Are you okay?"

Jensen nodded. "Yeah. I'm more than okay. I can't believe we're getting married again."

Toby chuckled. "There was no way my mom wasn't going to have a party to celebrate this. Plus, even though my sisters understood why we did it, they were upset they missed it. I had to promise them we'd do something big when you recovered from your trip."

"Your family loves you." Jensen nuzzled Toby's chest while petting his stomach.

"Of course they do. So much that it drives me crazy at times," Toby agreed.

Jensen's stubble-covered cheek rubbed over Toby's skin when he shook his head. "I mean everyone loves you, even your extended family. Usually there are members who don't want anything to do with the gay ones. Yet I haven't met any of those in yours."

Sighing, Toby said, "Trust me. There are those in my family, but my mom and dad don't invite them to our parties. My mom has always said that life is too short to deal with mean people. So she doesn't and my dad follows her example."

He ran his hand along Jensen's spine, tracing each vertebra before moving on to the next. Jensen shivered when Toby teased the soft skin at the top of his crease.

"How long have you been having these nightmares?" Toby kept his voice low, not wanting to act as if it was a big deal.

"Since about a week after I got back from Nepal," Jensen confessed. "They aren't that bad, really. Just shake me up a little bit until I make sure you're still there next to me then I can go back to bed. I only have them once a night."

Toby hummed for a few seconds while he thought. "I wonder why you're having them."

Shrugging, Jensen teased Toby's belly button, drawing a laugh from him. "I don't know. Nothing bad happened on the climb. I mean there were injuries, but nothing serious and no one died this season on the mountain. Just something I'll work through. It hasn't kept me from getting enough sleep."

"Did you want to go talk to someone about them?" He wasn't sure how Jensen would react to that suggestion. Jensen had never struck Toby as the introspective therapy type kind of guy.

He was sure there was a lot of that kind of looking inward while climbing a mountain that could kill you, but when Jensen was home, he seemed content with the life they had.

"If they get worse—or start to cause me to lose sleep—I'll go. I think it's just a reaction to being away for so long and all that." Jensen encircled Toby's waist. "Do we have to get up now?"

Toby was glad that his lover seemed to be willing to get help if things got worse. He twisted to get another look at the clock.

"We've got another hour and a half before we have to get up. You can nap." Massaging Jensen's shoulders, he hoped he would fall back to sleep. While Jensen had recovered for the most part, he was still tired at times, so Toby tried to encourage naps and sleeping in.

"Okay. Thanks."

Jensen breathing deepened and Toby waited until Jensen rolled over on his side away from him before he climbed out. He was wide-awake and wouldn't be going back to sleep any time soon. He might as well check on the stock market before taking a shower and making sure their bags were in the car for the trip.

The stocks were fine, nothing for him to panic about, so he wandered to their bathroom to turn on the shower. He shaved while water heated up then stepped in. He usually took short showers unless Jensen joined him. Then they could spend as long as the hot water lasted — touching, fucking and whatever else they felt like doing.

He dried off, tossing his towel and the one he'd used earlier into the hamper. After dressing in khaki cargo shorts and a blue T-shirt, he brushed a kiss over Jensen's brow before heading downstairs to make some coffee.

An hour later, he looked up from the newspaper he was reading to watch Jensen stroll into the kitchen.

"Do you want some breakfast?" Jensen called out to where Toby sat on their deck.

"Yeah. We probably should eat something. We have about a five-hour drive to get to my parents' place. Mom will have lunch ready for us when we get there, so there's no stopping on the way. I packed a cooler with sodas and some snacks for the trip." He stood then gathered up the paper and his cup. "I'll make waffles. Do you want to make the eggs and bacon? Also, there's coffee already brewed."

Jensen came over to give him a peck on the lips before he started pulling out the eggs and bacon from the refrigerator while Toby poured out some more coffee into his cup. He enjoyed watching Jensen move around their kitchen and if he didn't get his ass in gear, there wouldn't be any waffles.

He got out all the ingredients and the waffle iron while Jensen got to scrambling the eggs. They worked silently but well together, touching as they passed each other, stealing kisses while waiting for the food to cook.

When all of it was done, they split it between their plates and filled a carafe with coffee before wandering out to the table. After settling in his chair, Toby took a bite of his eggs and groaned. Jensen chuckled.

"You're such a sucker for well-cooked food," Jensen teased.

"If I wasn't already married to you, I'd totally steal you away and keep you prisoner in my house to cook for me every day," Toby told him.

Jensen took a sip of his coffee before saying, "I wouldn't fight you, that's for sure. I love our kitchen. You did a great job picking out a house while I was gone to climb Mount Fuji, Especially without really even knowing what I wanted in a home."

Toby shrugged, pleased as always when Jensen complimented him on the house he'd chosen for them. "I just tried to remember what you said you wanted, plus I knew you liked to cook. You did realize that we never did get that dog you said you wanted."

"Yeah. We got distracted the weekend we were planning on going to the shelter. After that, things just go busy." Jensen shot him a look. "Would you like to go when we get back from our honeymoon?"

"Yes. If we get a dog, it'll give me something to take care of while you're gone to K2 next year." Toby shook his head. "I didn't handle myself well this last time."

He'd told Jensen about his working late all the time and getting drunk one night. Jensen had understood about the whole situation and had thanked Simpson again for taking care of Toby. It was fun to watch his best friend and his husband slowly come to a mutual understanding and a budding friendship. Toby had kept up the Friday dinners with his friends, who had taken Jensen back into their circle without a problem. Jensen enjoyed cooking for them, and their card games were quite competitive.

"A dog will keep you company, especially since it looks like Simpson won't have a lot of free time for much longer, if Cindi has her way." Jensen wiggled his eyebrows and Toby laughed.

"Oh my God, do you think she'll make him bring her?" Toby covered his mouth trying to stop from laughing any more. "Kelly and Wendy can't stand her."

"Hell, Simpson can't stand her, but she's like plastic wrap—the clingy kind. I'm afraid she's going to boil a bunny in his kitchen." Jensen rolled his eyes. "I can't believe she tried to come to our card night last week."

Toby groaned. "Oh, I know. Well, if she shows up at my parents', we'll let the girls take care of her. She'll get the point after talking to them."

Jensen snorted. "I wouldn't sic your sisters on anyone, not even Cindi."

"It might be the only way Simpson can get free of her." Toby finished his breakfast, licking the syrup from his fork. He heard a moan and glanced up to see Jensen staring at his tongue. He made more of a production of cleaning the utensil, just to watch Jensen's face flush with desire.

"Stop teasing. You know we have to leave if we're going to get to your parents on time." Jensen mock snarled at him before getting up to stack their plates.

"I'll make it up to you tonight," Toby promised, as he joined him in the kitchen.

They cleaned up then Toby went through the house, making sure the windows and doors were locked and all the lights were off. When he was done, he met Jensen outside.

"I gave Jackie the key and our number. She said she'd pick up our mail and keep an eye on things," Jensen informed him as they climbed into the car.

Jensen was going to take the first leg of the drive then once they got into Vermont, Toby would take over to get them to his parents' place.

"Great. I like her and her kids." Toby buckled his seat beat then wiggled to find just the right spot.

"I do too."

Jensen started the vehicle then pulled out of the driveway. Toby relaxed as he rolled down his window and turned up the radio. He loved road trips, especially when it was with someone he adored.

Chapter Fifteen

Love is when he gives you a piece of your soul, that you never knew was missing.

— Torquato Tasso

Jensen braced himself when he stepped from the car. The onslaught of children heading toward him was enough to make a special ops soldier turn tail and run. He fell back against the side of the vehicle when two of the kids hit his legs while the other two grabbed his hands and started tugging.

"Uncle Jensen, where's our presents?"

"Uncle Jensen, what's you get us from the mountain?"

"Uncle Jensen, what was it like?"

"Uncle Jensen, will you come to my class and be my show-and-tell?"

Four voices all talking at the same time, asking him a dozen questions. He had to laugh because there was no way he could answer them until they shut up. So he hugged each boy, hoping Toby or their parents would rescue him.

"What am I now? Chopped liver?" Toby came around the front of the car and pouted. "Just because he climbed the world's tallest mountain doesn't mean he's Iron Man or anyone cool like that."

Toby winked at him when the boys protested that Jensen was way cooler than Iron Man. They rushed Toby and climbed all over him as well, hugging and asking him what he'd brought them.

"God, you little beggars, at least let them get inside before you start demanding presents." Kelly strolled from the house. It was obvious she was Toby's sister with the blonde hair and blue eyes they'd inherited from their mother and the slender build they got from their dad.

Jensen went over to where she stood and swept her into a big hug. She embraced him back, tight for a moment before loosening up. After setting her down, he frowned at her.

"Sorry. I'm just so glad to see you and that nothing happened while you were over there." She smiled. "It would've destroyed all of us if something had gone wrong."

He wasn't going to dismiss her concern, just like he hadn't done that with Toby before he'd left. "It was unseasonably good weather this season. We were lucky there wasn't anything bad. Thank you for being worried about me."

She punched him in the arm. "Of course, we worry about you. You're our brother-in-law now, and even if you never got married, Toby loves you, so that makes you family."

"She's right," Wendy agreed as she stepped out on to the front porch.

Jensen hugged her before greeting Bill and Shane, the ladies' husbands. Then Toby's parents came out and

Nancy squeezed him so hard that he thought he might break a rib if she didn't let up.

"Mom, you're going to injure him," Toby protested with a laugh. "Let him go. He's fine. You've seen him since he's been home." Toby brushed a kiss over his mom's cheek while tugging her away from Jensen.

"I'm glad you made it home without any injuries," Toby's dad said, giving him a quick hug then shaking his hand. "You're looking a lot better than the last time we saw you."

Jensen nodded. "I'm feeling better too, sir."

"Now, Jensen, what did I tell you?"

"Sorry, Dad." They exchanged smiles before Jensen returned to the car to help Toby carry their luggage inside.

"Toby, you and Jensen are in your usual room," Nancy told them, waving her hand toward the stairs.

Nodding, Toby led the way upstairs where they dumped their bags. Jensen was pretty sure Toby would end up unpacking for them before the night was over and he didn't mind. They were going to spend three days with the family then head out on their honeymoon. Toby still hadn't said where they were going, but Jensen found he didn't need to know. As long as Toby was with him, every place was paradise.

"Take this," he told Toby after digging through his duffle for some things.

Toby took the scrapbook they'd put together of all the pictures Jensen took while on his trip. He'd also written down memories and thoughts he'd had during his trip and put them in there as well. They figured Toby's dad would love looking at the pictures.

Jensen gathered all the brightly wrapped presents he'd brought for everyone then motioned for Toby to head out. Toby shook his head as they walked down the hallway.

"You spoil all of them," he told Jensen with a scowl. Then ruined it when he leaned in to kiss him. "Thank you for loving my family."

"Thank you for sharing them with me."

Everyone was in the backyard, putting the finishing touches on the rose arbor they were going to get married under. The kids were running around, screaming and shoving each other, but as far as Jensen could tell, no one was getting hurt.

"The yard looks amazing, Dad." Toby slung his arm over Donald's shoulder. "We really appreciate you all going to so much trouble to do this for us."

Nancy poked Toby in the side. "It's no trouble at all. We did it for your sisters. Why wouldn't we do this for you?"

Toby shrugged and Jensen knew what he was thinking. No matter how accepting a family was of a loved one being gay, that didn't always translate to them being willing to show the entire world. Yet Jensen wasn't surprised that Toby's family went all out for this wedding. They were the kind of people who loved hard and were fiercely loyal to their members. That meant having a wedding for their gay son and inviting everyone they knew, not caring if some of those people accepted it or not.

"I know a few of your friends aren't coming because they don't believe in gay marriage," Toby said.

Donald snorted. "Then they aren't our friends any more, Toby. If they can believe in my daughters' weddings, then they can damn well believe in my son's. Doesn't matter who you marry."

Jensen nodded then held up the pile of presents in his arms. "I have stuff," he announced and the children came running.

He passed everything out then sat next to Toby, watching as they all ripped the paper to get at the gifts. The kids all received child-size bow and arrows. Kelly wrinkled her nose at him and he pointed out that the arrows had rubber tips. They weren't dangerous.

The ladies got the most beautiful scarves Jensen had ever seen, created with bright colors that he'd picked specifically for each of the women. He'd bought leather wallets, etched with gorgeous scrollwork for Bill and Shane. He gave Donald a Buddhist prayer flag like one he could've left up on Everest if he'd wanted.

Jensen hadn't bought Toby anything. His present to his husband had been the notebooks he'd filled with letters.

"Oh Jensen, this is amazing," Nancy exclaimed, running her hands over the scarf.

He got hugs from the ladies and backslaps from the guys. Toby handed him the scrapbook.

"I thought you might like to see my pictures from my trip." He held the book up.

"Yes." Donald grabbed for it. "You hadn't finished downloading them when we visited last."

Jensen watched as his family gathered around the table where Donald was then he went to join them as they started asking him about who the people were in the photos. He didn't know how much time had passed while he told stories about his trip, but finally Toby spoke up.

"All right, guys. Why don't we have lunch? You all can talk more about this tonight after the rehearsal dinner." Toby clapped his hands, drawing the kids' attention.

"Right. I thought we could have hamburgers and hot dogs for lunch then tonight we'll go to a really nice restaurant here in town. The chef there is amazing." Nancy got everyone moving toward the house.

Jensen picked up the scrapbook before going inside. After setting it down, he went to where the others stood around Nancy, getting their orders for helping with lunch. They chatted as they went about their appointed tasks. It was nice to be included in their conversation.

The first time he'd come to visit Toby's family, he hadn't known how to react to them. He'd never been part of a group like them. Not even Jigger and Cat were as boisterous and nosy as this family. He'd been nervous as well, not wanting Toby's parents to hate him because he knew it would've broken his lover's heart if he'd had to choose between them.

Luckily that didn't happen and Jensen had found himself sucked into the love. Sure, Toby and his sisters fought like siblings did, and while he never saw them do it, he was sure Nancy and Donald argued. Both were strong people who had their own opinions.

"Jensen, when are Cat and Jigger getting in?" Nancy asked while chopping up lettuce for the salad.

"First thing tomorrow. They couldn't get an earlier flight and Cat refused to let Jigger charter one." He laughed at the dressing down Jigger had gotten for even suggesting it.

"I can't believe I'm going to get to meet Jigger Richeleau," Kelly squealed like a schoolgirl.

"He's not that Jigger anymore," Jensen reminded her, not wanting her to be disappointed when she met him. "He's really toned down. Rehab and fatherhood can do that to a guy."

"So true. Marriage and fatherhood does steal away your reckless youth," Bill said mournfully.

"Hey there." Kelly glared at him, hands on her hips.

He swooped in to kiss her. "And I don't regret giving it up."

Everyone laughed and Kelly asked Jensen about some of his other climbs. He talked about Fuji and Denali. They listened as he described some of his more harrowing climbs, but he always tried to downplay the danger he'd been in. No point in freaking Toby before he had to.

"Jensen and I are going to adopt a dog when we get back from our honeymoon," Toby announced, which led to an in-depth discussion on the best kind of dog to get and which breeds were better suited for where they lived.

"You'll want one that likes kids," Nancy told them.

"Of course. The kids will be visiting during the summer like this year and we'll make sure the dog won't be upset by them," Jensen reassured her.

"There is that, but you'll want a kid-friendly one for when you start adopting."

The way she said it was so nonchalant that Jensen frowned for a moment while he tried to make sense of what she'd said. He shot Toby a glance and Toby shrugged his shoulders before flashing him a rueful smile.

"She's started already. I would've thought you'd at least wait until after the ceremony tomorrow, Mom," Wendy spoke up from where she sat, feet up and her hands resting on her extended belly. "Plus I'm giving you another grandchild. You shouldn't be so greedy."

"They've been married six months, Wendy. It's time they begin thinking about adding to their family, and I don't mean a dog." Nancy turned to eye both of them. "You'll be wonderful fathers and there are a lot of children out there who need parents who love them. It doesn't matter that you're two men. All that matters is that you'll give those children the best life possible."

Toby took his mom's hand in his. "Mom, we've talked about it, but I would like to wait a little while longer. Jensen's going to Pakistan to climb K2 next year. I'm not sure getting a child then having Jensen gone for so long would be a good idea."

Shane spoke up. "You wouldn't get a child that quick. It can take up to a year or longer to be approved to adopt then to find the right kid."

"See." Nancy nodded in Shane's direction. "He's right. You should get the process started. By the time Jensen gets back, you should be approved and can start going through the selection process."

"Maybe they want to get a surrogate instead of adopting, Mom. Some guys want kids of their own blood instead of someone else's," Bill interjected.

Toby shot Jensen a worried glance and Jensen smiled. Hell, he didn't care where the kids came from, he just wanted to raise them with Toby in their home. In a way, he'd rather adopt children that were abandoned — or orphaned — than have one with his own DNA. He knew what it was like to not be wanted by his parents.

"Mom," Toby said and waited until she looked at him before he continued, "Jensen and I will talk about this when we feel we're ready. I know you would like more grandchildren, but you have to remember something. We might have been married for six months, but we haven't lived together for most of those six months, not that I think being married will change anything."

"We just need time to readjust how we think of things before we throw kids into the mix," Jensen spoke up. He definitely wasn't saying no to adding to their family.

She seemed content with that answer, though he figured they'd be hearing more about it as the months rolled on.

"Lunch is ready," Donald announced and they went outside to circle the large picnic table.

* * * *

Jensen snuggled close to Toby under the blankets. The air conditioning kept their room cold and he was having a bit of a flashback to Base Camp. Thankfully, Toby wasn't interested in pushing him away. He moaned a little when Toby ran his hand down his back to tease the small spot at the top of his crease.

"I'm sorry about my mom pushing for kids," Toby murmured.

Jensen eased back far enough he could look up into Toby's eyes. "Don't be. She loves you and just wants you to have a happy family."

"And since she's happily married, she wants the same thing for all her children." Toby gave him a small smile. "She did the same thing to my sisters when they got married. Like at the reception, she was asking them when they planned on starting their families."

"You know my thoughts and opinions on it. Maybe we should start the process when we get back from our honeymoon. This time I don't have to fly out to Pakistan until June. I'll make a few trips out to Wyoming, and meet up with Jigger for some fourteen thousand foot climbs in Colorado. We'll also do a lot of rock climbing, since there are a few more technical challenges on K2. Maybe we'll be approved before I go." He cradled Toby's face with both hands and rubbed his thumb over Toby's bottom lip.

"So you won't be gone as long as you were for Everest?" Toby stuck his tongue out to lick the pad of Jensen's thumb.

"I'll be gone for around a month and half or so. It should take us up to forty days to climb the mountain, but that's as long as we get good weather." Jensen leaned up to meet Toby's kiss. He didn't want to talk about K2 yet. They had several months before his trip.

He had other things to do, like make love to his husband.

Chapter Sixteen

Love knows not distance; it hath no continent; its eyes are for the stars.

— Gilbert Parker

Toby dropped his bags on the floor by their bed then collapsed face down onto the mattress. He was so freaking exhausted and so happy to be home. As much as he enjoyed his honeymoon with his husband, they had been so busy with exploring and visiting friends that he was tempted to call in sick tomorrow just so he could sleep in.

"Toby, are you awake?" Jensen strolled into the room, setting his own bags with Toby's before coming to sit next to him. Running his hand over Toby's hair, he chuckled. "Jet lag catching up with you?"

"I could sleep for two days," he muttered as he rolled over to nestle up against Jensen's thigh.

Jensen trailed his fingers over Toby's eyebrows then down the slope of his nose. "Why don't you take a nap?

I'll call Mom and let her know we got back okay. I also have to call Jigger, see how they're doing."

After sitting up, he started stripping off his clothes. "Don't let me sleep too long, or I won't be able to tonight."

"Don't worry. I'll take care of you."

He crawled under the blankets then wrapped his arms around one of their pillows. He felt Jensen brush a kiss over his temple before he drifted off.

* * * *

Two hours later, he climbed out of the shower to towel down. He dressed in the sweats and T-shirt Jensen had left out for him, plus the thick fuzzy socks he liked to wear around the house. He padded downstairs to find Jensen sitting outside, staring at the night sky. Coffee had been made, so he detoured to get a cup before he went to Jensen.

After pushing his chair back from the table, Jensen patted his thighs. "Sit."

Toby settled in Jensen's lap, snuggling close while sipping from his mug. They sat in silence for a few minutes, just absorbing the sounds of home. Then Toby's stomach growled and Jensen snickered.

"I take it you're hungry?"

"Yes. What do we have in the house or should we order in?" He didn't really want to move from where he was.

"Your mom came down yesterday to stock the refrigerator for us. I have some steaks marinating for the grill, plus there's asparagus for a side." Jensen nuzzled his hair and breathed in for a moment then he grabbed Toby around the waist to lift him up. He waited until Toby was balanced before he stood. "I'll get the food all ready. You just sit and drink your caffeine. Enjoy being home."

"Thank you." Toby took Jensen's chair, curling his feet under him to watch the fireflies zip among the flowers and bushes. He wasn't sure how long he sat there, but it was long enough for Jensen to get supper done.

He jumped a little when Jensen set a plate in front of him.

"Do you want a refill on your coffee?"

Shaking his head, he said, "I'm pretty sure if I have any more, I'll be up all night, even without the jet lag problem. I'll have water if you brought some out?"

"Yes, I did." Jensen placed a bottle next to Toby's plate. "The steak's just the way you like it. I grilled the asparagus as well."

Toby took Jensen's hand in his and kissed his knuckles. "I appreciate you taking care of me."

Jensen squeezed his fingers. "You did the same for me when I got home from Everest. It's what spouses do for each other."

He cleaned his plate while Jensen took time to eat his. Once he was done, he leaned back in the chair and watched Jensen. His husband winked at him when he took a drink.

"Your mom wants to know when we can come up and visit for the weekend. She wants to see our pictures from Australia and hear all about diving on the Reef." Jensen shook his head. "I can't believe you really took me to Australia for our honeymoon. It was great to see Rodney again."

"You two acted like you were long lost brothers," Toby said as he remembered how Rodney and Jensen had bragged about the different climbs they'd done.

The ones that were dangerous and the ones that were so easy a baby could have done them.

"He was the secondary guide on my trip and, climbing together, we got to be friends. I was thinking we should go visit him next year if he isn't doing an expedition. I figured sometime in February, since it'd be winter here." Jensen sat back and took a swig of water. "I guess we don't have to do that now."

"Oh we can still do it, if I have vacation days left." Toby shrugged. "If not, you could probably do it without me."

Jensen pursed his lips then shook his head. "No. I don't want to travel without you, except for my climbing trip. Once K2 is done, all the trips I go on after that will be with you and our kids."

Toby chuckled. "Why don't we get a dog first? Then work on the kids."

"Do you think Bill will help us get something set up? For the kids? I don't think we need a lawyer for the dog." Jensen wasn't sure how the whole process happened, but he'd like to put it in play if they could.

Thinking for a moment, he nodded. "I'm not sure he's qualified for that, but he'll know who we can go see to get it rolling."

Jensen grabbed him before pulling him to his feet, embracing Toby and pressing a kiss to his lips. Toby slid his hands into Jensen's hair, holding him still so Toby could devour his mouth.

He tasted the salty seasonings Jensen had put on their steaks, plus the underlying spice of Jensen himself. He caught Jensen's bottom lip in his teeth and tugged, loving the moan he got by doing that. Jensen grasped his ass and Toby knew what his husband wanted. He jumped up, wrapping his legs around Jensen's waist.

Somehow they managed to navigate the kitchen and the stairs. Toby was very impressed when they got to their bedroom with tripping over anything or getting hurt. Of course, he only thought that after they were done. While they moved, he was far more interested in kissing Jensen then how they got there.

"Omph!" Air rushed from him when Jensen dropped him on the bed.

"We should have gotten this out of our system while in Australia, but I can't get enough of you." Jensen fumbled with the waistband of Toby's sweats, tugging them off as quickly as he could.

Toby hadn't bothered with putting underwear on, so it was easy for him to spread his legs and Jensen to drop to his knees then swallow Toby down to the root. He shot up to grab Jensen's head.

"Holy shit!"

Jensen bobbed up and down while Toby lifted his hips in time with Jensen's movement. He groaned as Jensen took a hold of his balls, fondling them before slipping his fingers behind them to press against Toby's hole.

"The lube's in the nightstand," he reminded Jensen.

He snorted softly when Jensen shot him a glance.

"Right. Sorry. You are kind of busy and I don't want you to stop."

Toby twisted and wiggled until he could reach the drawer. He got it open then dug around to get his hand on the bottle. Yanking it out, he crowed in triumph. A snapping sound caught his attention and he saw Jensen holding his hand up.

"All right."

It took a little contorting, but he got it open to squirt some slick in Jensen's palm. Toby shut it then dropped it on the floor, not caring where it went. He fell back onto the bed then caught his legs behind the knees, dragging them up to expose his opening. Jensen moved with him and managed to keep his mouth on Toby's cock.

"Oh Christ," he moaned, as Jensen pressed two fingers into him. He was sore from all the sex they'd had on their trip, but not enough to stop Jensen from stretching him. "More."

Jensen thrust three in and nailed Toby's gland. When Toby jerked, Jensen winked at him then began to hit that same spot over and over until Toby cried out.

"Please." He rocked his hips asking for whatever Jensen was willing to give.

The suction around his cock grew stronger and Toby's balls drew tight to his body as his climax rolled over him. He flooded Jensen's mouth, shouting Jensen's name as he came.

He trembled as Jensen sucked him until he softened then licked him clean. Jensen didn't take his fingers out and Toby grunt when Jensen flexed them as he stood. Only then did Jensen ease them out before replacing them with his length.

"God, I can't get enough of you," Jensen mumbled when he bottomed out.

Toby took a hold of the sheets under him when Jensen started reaming his ass. He winced at how hard Jensen gripped him. Clenching around Jensen's shaft, Toby lifted just a little more and Jensen's eyes crossed.

"Fuck," he gasped.

"Yeah. Maybe you should get started with that," Toby joked then winked when Jensen glared at him.

Jensen pulled back until only his head was inside Toby then slammed back in, their shouts mingling together. It was only a few seconds before Jensen was fucking him as hard as he could. Toby hooked his ankles together behind Jensen's waist, doing everything he could to encourage him to come.

He watched as Jensen threw his head back and yelled then filled Toby's channel with cum. Toby kept massaging Jensen's length with his inner muscles, drawing every last drop from him that he could.

Toby opened his arms to embrace Jensen who collapsed on top of him. He ignored the semen coating his thighs when Jensen pulled out, satisfied to lay there with his husband until Jensen was ready to move.

Finally, Jensen inhaled deeply before pushing up on his hands to stare down at Toby. He brushed back the sweaty strands of hair from Jensen's forehead, smiling at him while he did so.

"We should go clean up," Jensen said.

Toby nodded. "Yeah. Ourselves and our dinner plates from the backyard."

Jensen grimaced. "Oh right. Forgot about that."

He chuckled as Jensen yawned then stood. After taking the hand Jensen offered him, Toby let him pull him to his feet. They meandered into the bathroom before taking a quick shower. Cleaning up their dinner went by just as fast and soon Toby found himself under the covers, wrapped in Jensen's embrace.

"What kind of dog are we looking for?" Jensen murmured, his lips moving against Toby's shoulder.

He shrugged. "I don't know. Do you have a preference? I think it would be cool to have one that I could take running when you're not here."

"So probably a bigger one?"

"Yeah, but we'll see what the shelter has to offer. I know I don't want to buy one from a breeder. Nothing wrong with that, but there are so many unwanted dogs in shelters. It'd be nice to give one a home."

"Like you did with me," Jensen said.

Toby frowned. "What are you talking about?"

Jensen sighed as though he wished he had never made that statement. "I wasn't in a shelter, but I spent most of my life unwanted. Yet for some reason, you saw something in me and ended giving me a home and loving me."

"That's because you're lovable, gorgeous and a nice person." Toby entwined their fingers, laying their hands over his heart. "I'm glad I can give you a home to return to, but you've also given me more than I ever imagined."

He smiled when Jensen simply kissed the nape of his neck in response. Jensen had given him the one thing Toby hadn't been sure he'd ever find. He'd given him a man he could love and that was no small feat.

Chapter Seventeen

*K2 is not some malevolent, lurking there above the Baltoro,
waiting to get us. It's just there. It's indifferent. It's an
inanimate mountain made of rock, ice, and snow. The
"savageness" is what we project onto it, as if we blame the
peak for our own misadventures on it.*

— Ed Viesturs

The soft beeping brought Jensen out of his restless
sleep. He reached to turn the clock off, but he gasped at
the pain when he tried to move his arm.

"Oh don't move, Jensen. Do you want something?"

He forced open his eyes to see Cat standing over him.
He blinked, trying to figure out why she'd be in his
bedroom.

"Jensen, what do you need?"

"Cat." He winced as how hoarse his voice was.

She held a cup with a straw for him to drink from and
the cool water hitting his throat made him moan. When
he had enough, he turned his head away. Cat set it
down then took his left hand in hers.

"Why are you in my bedroom?"

Her eyes widened when he asked. "Don't you remember what happened? You're in the hospital in Hartford. You've been here for three days."

Three days? Jensen glanced around, being careful not to move the rest of his body. The plain white walls and the machines told him she spoke the truth.

"I need to sit up," he said and Cat handed him the remote for his bed. As he raised himself up, he looked down to see the blanket covering his legs. Yet when he tried to move them, his left twitched, but all he felt was pain from his right.

He stared at his hands, finally noticing they were wrapped in bandages to the point where he could barely bend his fingers. When he saw that and glanced around to see his backpack sitting there, he remembered what had happened.

"I fell," he spoke aloud.

Cat swallowed as tears welled in her eyes. "Yeah."

Fear swept through him. "Where's Toby?" He twisted, searching the room. There wasn't anyone else except Cat there.

"Toby? Where is he?" Panic started to raise his heartbeat, making the heartbeat monitor speed up.

"Jensen, you need to calm down. Toby went to get something to eat. His mother dragged him out of here about ten minutes ago. I texted him, so they'll be back soon." Cat rested her hand on his thigh.

"Did I lose my leg or my fingers?" He held his hands up to show her the wraps. "I thought it was only broken. Did I get frostbite?"

Cat licked her lips, but before she could answer him, a nurse walked in. Jensen answered her questions, though he wanted her to go away so he could talk to Cat. By the time she was done, Toby rushed in.

"Oh my God, you're awake." Toby didn't hesitate to throw his arms around Jensen and pull him close as they could get with the bandages and machines in the way.

Jensen lifted his head, hoping Toby would understand what he wanted, since Jensen's throat seemed to have closed as soon as Toby had walked into the room. No matter what Cat had said, he couldn't help but think that Toby had left him. He was worried that Toby wouldn't have been able to handle that Jensen had been injured while climbing K2. It was the one thing Toby had always been afraid of happening. Hell, Toby had been scared Jensen would die.

Toby pressed his lips to Jensen's, breathing in his sob and letting it mingle with his. Jensen whimpered, wishing he could touch Toby's skin, his hair, and his face, but the bandages wouldn't allow him. It was as if Toby understood because he took Jensen's face in his while they kissed.

When he couldn't breathe anymore, he broke their embrace, just enough to inhale deeply. Then he snuggled closer to Toby.

"I'm sorry," he muttered. "I'm so sorry."

Toby nudged him until he leaned back and Toby could meet his gaze. "There's nothing to be sorry for, love. You didn't do it on purpose. I know that."

"I took a step then I fell." Jensen shot a glance at Cat. "Is Jigger okay? He was right behind me when I fell. He was hooked to the rope like me. Did my weight pull him down with me?"

Worry rocketed through him when they didn't answer right away, but Cat shook her head. Toby cleared his throat, bringing Jensen's attention back to him.

"No. Jigger's fine. He's at the house, watching Pammy and Coop for us. Now that you're awake, he'll be by to see you later." Toby took a hold of Jensen's elbow since he couldn't do anything with his hands. "He told us what happened."

"I was just going down the ridge. We'd gone up the same way. There shouldn't have been anything wrong. It should've been safe." Jensen started panting as he thought about how close he'd come to dying on that mountain.

Toby rested his forehead against Jensen's. "Breathe with me, Jensen. In and out. In and out," he said softly, inhaling deeply and slowly exhaling.

He stared into Toby's eyes, doing as his husband ordered. His panic began to ease and the bands around his chest loosened.

"I'd like to check him out, if he's okay?"

When Toby stepped back, a doctor stood with a slight smile on his face. He didn't want Toby to let go of him and Toby must have figured that out.

"I'll be right here where you can see me," Toby told him. "I'm not leaving."

Every time he looked, Toby was right where he'd promised he'd be and Jensen was relieved. He'd been so afraid that Toby would leave him after he got hurt, even though he still didn't remember the whole event.

The doctor checked his eyes and everything while talking to him. Then he lifted the blanket to look at Jensen's leg. When he saw the large white cast around it, Jensen drooped in his bed.

"I didn't lose it," he whispered.

"Oh no. You broke the femur and the tibia on your left leg." The doctor tapped the cast. "It'll take you a while to heal, but the surgeons were able to put screws and a plate in. You'll have a limp and probably know when it's going to storm."

Jensen held up his hands. "What about these?"

"Those are going to be tricky. You got burns across your palms. As you fell, you must have grabbed a hold of the rope and it tore through your gloves. Plus you have frostbite on all the fingers on your right hand. Not sure how that happened, though it could've been pulled off when you fell. From what I understand, it was rather cold where your accident happened, as well as you were in the middle of a freak snowstorm. It took your friends time to get to you."

Toby whimpered and Jensen reached for him. The doctor moved out of the way, seeming to understand how Toby was feeling. Jensen did the best he could to wrap his arms around Toby, not caring about the wires and IVs. Toby buried his face in Jensen's neck and whimpered again.

"You're doing well. I'll stop by tomorrow. Have the nurse call me if you have any questions or problems." The doctor patted his leg then left.

Jensen met Nancy's concerned gaze over Toby's head and gave her a weak smile. He wished he could offer her his hand to hold, but that was impossible with the injuries he'd suffered. She touched his blanket-covered right foot and he got that she knew what he was thinking.

"Cat, why don't you and I go grab some supper for Toby? That way he can eat in here with Jensen," Nancy suggested.

"Sounds good. Actually I could use something to eat as well." Cat gave him a quick kiss before leaving with Nancy.

Once the ladies were out of the room, he eased Toby away from him and frowned when he couldn't wipe the tears off Toby's face. Toby chuckled softly then swiped his sleeve over his cheeks to get rid of them.

"I'm sorry," Jensen said again.

Toby held up his hand. "Stop. Don't keep apologizing. You don't need to say you're sorry anymore for leaving all those years and you certainly don't need to apologize for this. This wasn't your fault. It was a simple accident that could've happened to anyone climbing that mountain."

He bit back another "I'm sorry" and exhaled in annoyance at the bandages on his hands. "How am I supposed to do things with these?"

Taking Jensen gently in his hands, Toby bent to place a kiss on each of his palms. "Mom's going to stay for a little while until the bandages come off. Once that happens—as long as you take it easy—you should be able to use them just fine. The doctors say the wrappings can come off in a couple of days, but you won't be able to use them that much for another two weeks or so. You'll have rehab to get the muscles and tendons working again. The rope cut really deep."

As much as he hated the thought of someone taking care of him, he knew that Toby wouldn't be able to take that much time off to do it. They'd deal with Toby's mom being there.

"What about my leg?"

Toby shrugged. "That'll be longer, but once your hands are better, it'll be easier for you to get around. Coop will learn not to trip you up. God, that dog is going to be so happy to see you. He's been missing you like crazy."

Jensen grinned. "I've missed him too, though not as much as I've missed you. I'm glad this was my last climb, especially now that I've done this." He motioned to all of his injuries.

After sitting on the edge of the bed, Toby studied him. "Do you remember all of what happened?"

"Not all of it. Did I hit my head too?" He went to touch the back of his head.

Toby caught him before he did anything. "Yes, you did, but it was a glancing blow. There's a bump there and I'm sure if you messed with it, it'd hurt."

Grimacing, he nodded. "You're probably right."

He glared down at his lap, not sure what he was feeling. There was pain from his hands and leg, plus he was sure he had bruises all over his body from his fall. There was definitely shock that something like this could've happened to him, but the odds were good that he was going to experience some kind of incident on a mountain the longer he continued to climb. Denali was his first and while he hadn't wanted to repeat what happened there, it looked like he had managed to have a worse accident, anger that he ended up hurt because of no fault of his own.

Not that he wanted to be the cause of the situation, but still maybe he would've been able to explain the events leading up to it if he knew exactly what had gone wrong. Yet the only thing he could blame was the one thing he couldn't control. K2 wasn't a forgiving mountain. It changed second to second, without giving notice. They had made their way up to the summit the same route as they'd come down.

"Ransom had set up two acclimatization climbs for us. We could've done it with just one, but we had the time and he didn't want to rush it. As much as I wanted to come home to you, I also was really enjoying being on the mountain." Jensen shot a quick glance at Toby to see how he reacted to that.

Toby nodded. "Of course you did. It would be like me going on a skiing trip without you. I'd love every minute of it, but I'd also really miss being with you."

He was glad Toby got what he was trying to say. "Right. I was getting some awesome shots and Jigger and I were doing great with the different climbs. Even the rock climbs, which aren't our strengths, were going well."

"What about weather? You didn't tell me about it when we talked, and Simpson forbid me to check the reports." Toby chuckled. "I have a tendency to obsess about that."

"No. Really?" He tried to move away before Toby could pinch him lightly on the side, but having a cast made him pretty much immobile. "We had good weather. It might have been too good. The sun at the upper levels of the mountain would melt the snow and ice, which is what I think could've caused me to fall."

A yawn caught him off guard and Toby's expression softened. He leaned in to trail his finger over Jensen's jaw before placing a kiss on his lips.

"Why don't you take a nap? Now that you've been awake for a while and the doctor has checked you over, I think you can get some uninterrupted sleep for a change." Toby stood then lowered the head of the bed slightly. He tucked Jensen in, pulling the blankets tight around him. "I'll be right here when you wake up and we'll talk some more."

Jensen nodded, suddenly unable to keep his eyes open. The last thing he saw before he fell asleep was Toby wiping another tear from his cheek while smiling down at him.

Chapter Eighteen

*We had forgotten that the mountain still holds the master
card, that it will grant success only in its own good time.*

— Eric Shipton

Toby raised his head from where he had laid it on his
arms. He'd been sitting next to Jensen's bed, watching
him sleep when his own exhaustion had swept over
him. Resting his arms on the edge of the mattress, he'd
put his head down and he must have fallen asleep.

He saw his mother, Cat and Jigger peek around the
door. Waving for them to come in, he stood then
stretched, cringing at the sound of his vertebra popping
as he moved. His mom gave him a quick hug as did Cat.
Jigger shook his hand.

"How's he doing?" Jigger tipped his head in Jensen's
direction.

"Good. The doctor said he'll be fine. It'll just take a
while to heal, but there won't be any lasting damage."
Toby had been so relieved to hear that. "He won't be a

hundred percent, but he won't lose any fingers, toes or his leg."

Jigger looked happy. "Good. Hey, we brought you some food."

Cat held up a bag and Toby's stomach growled. He hadn't eaten since that morning and after Jensen woke up for good, he had forgotten about getting a meal. Nancy cleared a spot for him off the little table in the corner.

"Who's watching Pammy and Coop?" he asked, as he sat and inhaled the smell of the clam chowder coming from the plastic container Cat put in front of him.

"Your father. He'll be by tomorrow to check on Jensen." Nancy patted his shoulder then began to putter around the room, straightening things.

"I appreciate everything you're doing for us, Mom." Toby snagged her wrist to pull her into a quick hug. "I'm not sure I'd be able to hold it together without your help—all of you." He included Cat and Jigger with his smile.

Jigger snorted. "Man, I was up there with him. I kind of feel responsible for the whole fucking accident."

Toby dropped his spoon into the soup before whirling to meet Jigger's guilty expression. "Why? Did you know the weakened snow covered a crevasse and chose not to tell Jensen? Did you shove him so that he fell?"

"No!" Jigger's eyes widened at those suggestions. "I'd never do that. I had no clue."

"Then it wasn't your fault. You got to him as fast as you could and did everything you could to keep him safe and alive until you could get to the hospital." Toby gripped Jigger's arm and squeezed. "Trust me. He doesn't blame you for any of it, and I certainly don't."

Jigger didn't seemed convinced and Toby figured he would have to hear it from Jensen himself before he started letting go of that guilt. And he might always feel like he could've done something differently to keep Jensen from getting hurt. It was something everyone did when friends were injured.

"Is that clam chowder?"

They all swung around when Jensen spoke. Nancy bustled over to help him sit up and gave him a hug when she was done. Jigger went over and the two friends shared a silent moment staring into each other's eyes.

"I'm sorry, man," Jigger murmured.

Jensen shook his head. "There's nothing to be sorry for. I remember hearing you shout around the same time as the ledge went out from under me. Was there a crack — or something — that you heard to make you do that?"

Jigger swallowed as he nodded. Cat shoved the chair to him and he took a seat. Toby went back to working on the supper they'd brought for him. He listened as they talked.

"Yeah. To be honest, I had a strange feeling when we reached that section, but I couldn't put my finger on what was throwing me off." Jigger hung his head. "Maybe if I'd said something, Ransom would've had us take a different line down."

"Nah." Jensen tapped Jigger on the head then grimaced as pain must have hit him. "I felt the same thing, but I thought it was just me being weird because everything had gone well on K2 and Everest. I should've known not to jinx us like that."

Cat giggled. "We're all superstitious when it comes to climbing, so yeah, you probably shouldn't have thought that."

"It's as though the climbing gods are watching and the moment you think you're home free, they throw shit at you just to laugh as you fumble along trying to figure out how the hell you're going to get out of it," Jigger explained to Toby and Nancy.

"Makes sense," Toby commented. He scooted his chair across the floor so he was closer to Jensen.

Jensen met his gaze, giving Toby a glimpse of how tired and in pain he was. Toby wished he could take it all away from Jensen, but there wasn't anything he could do. Both the tiredness and the pain would fade after a while. It would simply take time.

"How were the two acclimatization climbs? Those went fine, right?" He thought maybe going through the whole trip would help Jensen settle what went on in his mind.

"It took us seven days to get to the K2 base camp from Askole. We trekked in and Jensen got some awesome shots of the mountain wreathed in clouds. It got even more amazing every day we got closer to it. Weather was good and we didn't have any problems getting over the Baltoro glacier to camp." Jigger's excitement infused his voice. Toby could only imagine what he'd been like during the trip if he was still so thrilled about it afterward.

He watched as Jensen seemed to perk up, his eyes lighting with an almost fanatical glow.

"After two rest days, we started working on setting up the higher camps, plus getting used to the altitude. The first real challenge was the House's Chimney between Camp One and Camp Two." Jensen stopped for a moment as though he were remembering it. "It's a pretty much straight vertical crack that you have to go through to get to Camp Two."

"The second bitch of a climb is the Black Pyramid, which is what you have to negotiate the entire way between Camp Two and Camp Three. That one is a killer for sure, if you don't know what you're doing or don't take your time. While we're doing this, we're also working on establishing the fixed ropes for the climbs and summit push. So there's a lot going on and you have to pay attention." Jigger picked up Jensen's backpack that had come to the hospital with him from the airport when they flew him home from Pakistan. "I think your camera's still in here. We can show you some pictures of the climbs."

Jensen wiggled around until he faced Toby and Nancy. "See the difference between K2 and Everest is there is way more rock climbing involved with K2. It's not easy stuff either. It's some of the most difficult I've ever done in my life. Add into that, the crazy weather, fear of avalanche and rock falls, and K2 is one of the deadliest out there."

Toby knew how lucky there were that all Jensen suffered was a broken leg, a bump on the head and some light frostbite. He thanked God and every other deity he could think of every night since Jensen had gotten back to the states for bringing him home alive.

"As terrible as the whole experience was, Jensen's one of the lucky ones to get off the mountain alive." Jigger shrugged when Nancy glowered at him. "I'm just saying, ma'am. What happened could've been a lot worse."

"Right. I was lucky that I was almost back to Base Camp when I fell. If it had occurred farther up the mountain, I could've lost my fingers — or even my hands — to frostbite. If the wounds had gone gangrenous, then there wouldn't have been anything the doctors could've done to save them. Plus it's a bitch having to haul someone down from the upper camps to Base camp. Something like that could have disastrous consequences for everyone involved."

Clearing his throat, Toby dropped his gaze to the floor, not wanting to think about all the things that could've gone wrong during Jensen's rescue. He didn't need any more nightmares. He saw Jensen's bandages come into view and he looked up to see Jensen watching him. Trying to give him a smile, Toby admitted his attempt was pretty weak.

"But I didn't because Jigger, Ransom and the other guys were there to haul my ass out of the crevasse and get me down to Base Camp. Then Jigger chartered a helicopter to get me to the hospital at the one of the Pakistani military bases."

Jigger rolled his eyes. "Having money helps with being able to rescue people. Christ! You would think they'd have done it out of the goodness of their hearts, but no. I had to grease everyone's palms until we got to Germany."

Cat sighed. "Yeah. It was so much fun coordinating that trip."

"Let me know how much it cost," Jensen informed them. "I'll pay you back for it."

"I don't think so," Jigger protested. "You don't owe me anything. I know you'd do the same for me if I needed to get my ass flown somewhere."

Toby could see that Jensen was going to argue and he knew Jigger wasn't going to accept any money from Jensen. He made a mental note to talk to Cat to see if there was a way they could reimburse them without insulting either man's pride. Maybe they could put the money in Pammy's education fund, though it wasn't like Jigger didn't have enough money to send ten children to college.

"When did you decide to go to the summit," he interjected, not wanting them to get mad at each other.

Both men frowned as they thought about it. Cat bumped Toby's shoulder, mouthing 'Thank you' to him and he grinned. She obviously didn't want them fighting either.

"Around our fourth week there. We'd spent four days in Base Camp after going up to Camp Three and back for our last acclimatization climb. Ransom had an eye on the weather, which was clear and wasn't supposed to get any better than it already was. God, it was fucking cold though." Jigger shuddered. "I must be getting older because it was cutting right through my jacket and when I got back here, I never thought I was going to get warm again. Still get chilled from time to time."

"Tell me about it." Jensen motioned to the three blankets he had covering him. "I think I might need another one before I go to bed tonight."

"I can go ask the nurse for one," Nancy offered then she left.

"It's not as bad as Everest was. Maybe because we didn't spend as much time on the actual mountain. Just one night at each camp on our way to the summit, then one night at Camp Three on the way down." Jigger pursed his lips as though he was working out whether that assumption was right or not.

"We set out for the summit from Camp Four at like eleven o'clock at night then hit the Bottleneck Couloir. That was brutal, full of rocks and ice. There are other ways to circumvent that area, but once Ransom had a good look at them, he decided the best thing was just to take the normal route because none of them were particularly safe." Jensen continued the story. "So we pushed on to the summit and made it there around eight the next morning. There's nothing in the universe like standing at twenty-eight thousand two hundred and fifty-one feet and looking out over the world."

Jigger and him shared a smile and Toby felt a little hint of jealousy. He would never know what that feeling was like, never know the sense of accomplishment climbing the world's tallest mountains could bring a man. Yet when Jensen caught his gaze, Toby realized that didn't matter. Climbing made Jensen happy and helped him grow strong enough to keep away from the drugs. It gave him the high he needed to enjoy life without killing him. Toby hesitated at that thought. Well, without killing him slowly. If he were killed during a climb, it would more than likely be quick — or at least Toby hoped it would be quick.

"Here. These are the pictures from the summit. We didn't stay very long. Maybe fifteen minutes tops. It was freaking cold up there." Jigger handed him Jensen's camera.

Cat stepped closer as Toby scrolled through the pictures. There was a great one of Jigger grinning at the camera, holding up a sign that said, 'I love you, Cat'. Her breath caught at that and Toby decided to have it printed and framed for her. It was just like the one Jensen had taken at the top of Everest that Toby had hanging over their fireplace in his study at home. Jensen held a sign that said 'I love Toby'. When he'd seen it, he had tears in his eyes. It was Jensen's way of letting him know that Toby was never far from his thoughts.

There were more photos showing the beauty of K2, which seemed to hide the true danger of the mountain. That was the truth that made the tallest mountains so alluring to humans. Their beauty told lies to the people who wanted to climb them. It said that there was nothing difficult about scaling the slopes and walls, yet danger was around every rock and crack, under ice seracs and simple snowdrifts.

Jensen was proof of that and how the mountain could change in a matter of mere minutes. What once was the safest path down could become the deadliest. Toby shook his head, letting that thought go. His husband wasn't going to be climbing any more mountains – at least not 'the eight thousanders'. He wasn't entirely sure he wanted Jensen to climb at all, not even the ones that were mere hills in comparison to K2 and Everest.

"Once we were done, we headed down to Camp Three where we spent the night. Now we did all of this without supplemental oxygen. So by the time we got to our tents at the camp, we were exhausted. We climbed into our sleeping bags and had our tea, water and soup to try and warm up. Our porters had chosen to stay at the lower camp. They didn't want to summit." Jigger sounded as if he couldn't believe the men who were their support staff hadn't wanted to climb to the top.

"Is that normal? I thought the Sherpas always wanted to summit, and were quite disappointed if they were chosen to stay at camp," Toby asked, remembering what Jensen had told him about Everest.

"Ah, but these aren't Sherpas. These guys are Pakistani HAPs – or high altitude porters. They don't look at K2 the same way as the ones in Nepal do about Everest. Different attitude." Jensen waved his hands around and Toby suppressed his smile at the image Jensen made as though he were a little kid wearing mittens. "They were very helpful for what they did, don't get me wrong – just not quite like the guys we dealt with elsewhere."

Jigger and Cat both nodded, having dealt with guides and porters all around the world. Toby would take his word for it.

"The next morning, we got up and moved out, heading down to Base Camp. I was in the lead with Jigger behind me and Ransom bringing up the rear. It was another clear day out, and while I had to be careful of solar radiation because of how clear it was, I felt good. Sure, I was still tired from the summit push, but it wasn't anything I couldn't handle. We passed some other climbers heading up for their own try at the top. I wished them best of luck. It looked like quite a few people would get to summit K2, which isn't always the case."

Jensen leaned back against his pillows and Toby could see that he was tiring. He made a little motion to Cat, who nodded.

"I think we should head back to Toby's, Jigger. Give Donald a break from Pammy for the rest of the night. We can come back in the morning." Cat gave Toby a hug then Jensen. "Now that you're out of the woods, we're going to head back to Wyoming in a couple of days. Toby's parents have you covered until you can get around on your own."

"Yeah. You don't need to stay here, watching me sleep and heal. It's probably as exciting as watching paint dry," Jensen teased as he hugged both of them.

Cat and Jigger were walking out when Nancy returned.

"We're going to back to the house," Jigger let her know.

"I'll go with you," she told them before bustling over to hug Jensen and give Toby a kiss. "The nurse will be bringing you another blanket. We'll see you boys in the morning."

They left as quietly as they'd arrived and while Toby was happy they'd come to visit with Jensen, he liked being alone with him.

"Are you driving back and forth from the house?" Jensen frowned. "If yes, you should've gone with them."

"No. I have a hotel room about a block from here. I've been going there to shower and get some sleep. I just wanted to be closer, in case something went wrong." He studied Jensen. "I talked to the doctor earlier. He said if your hands are still good as they are now, I can take you home in two days. Then I'm going to have to go back to work."

Jensen shifted as though he wanted to say something, but thought better of it. Toby used the knuckle of his right hand to lift Jensen's chin, so their eyes could meet.

"What do you want to say?"

After licking his lips, Jensen said, "I was thinking that I might start up a small investment firm out of the house. I thought you could go in on it with me as my partner. When we need to hire more people, we can always move to an office in town. That way you're not driving back and forth to the city every day, plus I'll have something to do with my education."

Surprise rocketed through Toby. "I thought you didn't like the whole stocks and investment business."

"That's not it exactly. I don't like how fast paced and competitive it can be. See, the thing is, I have more than enough money to not work another day in my life, but I can't do that. I need to be doing something. Just a small firm with a few clients. Nothing big. It would be nice to work from home and have you there with me." He cleared his throat. "Especially when the kids come."

Toby started. "Oh my God, I totally forgot to tell you. Bill said that all the proper forms are in order and we can start thinking about adopting at any point we want to. The adoption itself might take a while, but luckily, us being gay doesn't matter at all."

Jensen closed his eyes and sighed. "I didn't think it would, but you never can tell sometimes."

"I know." Toby brushed back the hair off Jensen's forehead. "Maybe we'll worry about a kid in about four or five months after your leg's healed. I'm not sure you'll be up to dealing with one in the house while you're rehabbing."

"Good idea," Jensen mumbled.

Toby didn't say anything else, letting the silence settle between them, knowing it would help Jensen fall asleep. Now that he knew Jensen was going to be okay, he could start planning the rest of their lives. Jensen's idea of them working together had merit. Toby would have to look into that a little later.

Chapter Nineteen

It is not the mountain we conquer but ourselves.

— Sir Edmund Hillary

Jensen dropped into the chair on the deck and groaned as he lifted his leg to rest it on the stool Toby had brought home one day. *Christ! It's been two months and I want to cut this cast off myself.*

"Only another week or so, then it'll come off," Toby spoke up as he walked out from the house, carrying two glasses of lemonade. "Then the real fun starts. You get to start rehabbing it."

He rolled his eyes. "I can just imagine how fun that is going to be. After going through that shit for my hands, I can't wait."

Toby seemed amused by his sarcasm. "You'll do it because you want to go running with Coop and me."

The mutt they'd adopted before Jensen had left for K2 stood from where he'd been lying in the shade to wander over to them. He rested his head on Jensen's leg, demanding to be petted and Jensen obliged him.

Coop was medium-sized but muscular. The people at the shelter had said he probably had some Staffordshire terrier and Mastiff in his bloodline somewhere, so Coop appeared intimidating, but was actually the sweetest dog Jensen had ever met.

One of the best things about Toby taking Coop on runs with him was that Jensen didn't have to worry about anyone messing with them. Just the dog's presence was enough to make anyone think twice about bothering Toby.

"True." Jensen hated the imposed non-activity. "Thank God, I have to lift weights now, or else I'd be gaining weight like crazy."

"It helps that you're making the meals and keeping them healthy," Toby pointed out. "I talked to Bill about getting business papers drawn up for our firm. He said they should be done in a week or two."

He caught Toby's hand and stopped him before he could walk back inside. Toby stood there, smiling at him with affection clearly showing on his face. "Thank you for throwing your lot in with me."

Toby threaded his fingers through Jensen's hair. "I threw my lot in with you the moment you came back to me, Jensen. This is not anything special. I think it's a great idea and we'll be able to make a go of it. Plus, like you said about your own money, I have more than enough to not work for the rest of my life too. So this isn't that big of deal. Isn't this what happens when you get married?"

He pushed up a little to meet Toby who leaned down to kiss him. When he settled back, he licked his lips, loving the taste of Toby on his tongue. "Thank you for marrying me. When I came back to you, I never imagined a life like this."

"What did you imagine?" Toby tipped his head to one side to study him.

Shrugging, Jensen stared at Coop who was still sitting next to his chair. "I guess I didn't really imagine anything except hoping that you would forgive me. I certainly never thought you'd take me back or love me enough to marry me."

Toby kissed him again then eased back to say, "Then you weren't dreaming big enough, love. Now I have to go get supper or it'll be cold and cold salmon is only good if it's smoked."

"In your opinion. Go on, but while we eat, I'll be dreaming about something else for afterward." He leered at Toby who rolled his eyes, but Jensen saw the lust burning in them.

"Did the doctor clear you for that?"

Jensen snorted. "I didn't need my doctor's permission to have sex with my husband."

Holding up his hand as though to say 'hold that thought', Toby went into the kitchen then returned with their plates. He'd already carried out the utensils and salad while Toby worked on the salmon.

"You didn't need his permission, but it's always good to make sure we aren't going to injure you more if we do something," Toby informed him before taking a bite.

"True." He ate a couple of forkfuls of salad while Coop flopped at his feet and sighed with obvious starvation.

"You aren't starving, you silly dog." Toby poked Coop with his toe. "Look at you. If the vet saw you, she'd say we'd have to put you on a diet. Not even the runs are making you svelte again."

Coop groaned as he rolled over, his four paws up in the air and tongue hanging out the side of his mouth. Both Jensen and Toby burst out laughing. Jensen relaxed while they ate and talked about the other things they'd done that day. When Toby had handed in his two-week notice, his boss tried to get him to stay by offering him a raise and a corner office. While it had been tempting, Toby said no, which told Jensen all he needed to know about how much Toby wanted their marriage to work.

Jensen had gone to physical therapy for his hands, plus went to search for some office space. He and Toby had decided that they needed to keep their work separate from their home, so they were going to rent a place for their business.

"I found a few buildings that might work for us. I told our realtor that we could look at them on Saturday," he explained, as they cleaned up. He moved slowly, but Toby didn't try to do anything for him. Jensen liked the fact that Toby didn't treat him like a complete invalid now that his hands were healed.

Once the kitchen was put back to rights, Jensen leaned against the counter then encircled Toby's waist to pull him close. Their lips meeting brought a deep sigh from him. They hadn't had full sex since his accident because Toby didn't want to hurt his injuries. Luckily there were other intimate things they could do while they waited.

Now it was time to feel Toby inside him again—or be inside Toby—however his husband wanted it. Jensen swept his tongue inside to tease Toby while slipping his hands down Toby's back to cup his ass. They rocked together and Jensen groaned when their erections rubbed against each other.

Panting, he eased a few inches away. "I think we need to move this upstairs."

Toby nodded. "Why don't you head on up and I'll lock the place up?"

It would take him longer to get upstairs, though he had gotten better at going up and down with his crutches. He started to thump his way to their bedroom while Toby took care of the rest of the house. Coop stayed downstairs like he usually did for the first part of the night.

Once in their room, Jensen moved as quickly as he could to strip and get situated on the bed. He made sure the lube was close at hand while he leaned against the headboard. It wasn't long before Toby strolled in, his gaze going directly to Jensen sprawled on the mattress, stroking his cock idly.

"Hmm...I never get tired of that sight," Toby muttered as he stripped, his own length rising from his pubes.

"Come here," Jensen ordered, crooking his finger at Toby.

There was no doubt Toby was eager for whatever they were about to do. Jensen shifted and wiggled until he was flat on his back with only his head propped up. Toby climbed over to put his knees on either side of Jensen's head then braced his hands on the wall above them.

Jensen licked a line along the underside of Toby's shaft, loving the salty musky flavor of his lover. He pressed the tip of his tongue to the little piece of flesh just under the flared head and Toby moaned. Once he did, Jensen wrapped his lips around it then sucked.

"Oh my God, I love your mouth," Toby informed him then pushed in.

He didn't argue, just scrambled his fingers in the sheets to find the slick. When he got a hold of it, he opened it while Toby slowly slid in and out of Jensen's mouth. Jensen squirted some on his fingers then let it drop back to the bed.

Jensen slipped his fingers down Toby's crease, caressing his hole then moving down to play with his balls before returning to push just a small bit of his fingers into Toby. He knew Toby didn't like a lot of stretching. For some reason, he liked the intense burn he felt when Jensen took him without it. He was okay with that, though he did his best to use a lot of lube, hoping that eased his entrance a little.

When he got two fingers all the way in, Toby rocked between them and Jensen's mouth. He twisted them, doing what he could to nail Toby's gland each time. As Toby's movements grew faster and rougher, Jensen managed to get more lube into Toby's ass.

"Jensen," Toby cried out, but Jensen wrapped the fingers of his other hand around Toby's length to keep him from coming. "Damn it, Jensen."

Jensen let his head drop back so he could speak. "I don't want you to come until I'm inside you."

Toby took a deep breath then nodded. "All right."

Before he could say anything, Toby shifted down his body then took his cock in his hand and impaled himself. Jensen grabbed a hold of Toby's hips but didn't move. Toby bit his bottom lip as he squeezed his channel around Jensen.

His eyes rolling back in his head at the tightness, Jensen whimpered, wanting to move yet not wanting to do it until Toby let him know he was ready for more. He ran his hands over Toby's sides and chest, hoping his touch soothed his lover.

Toby relaxed a little more, which caused Jensen to sink a little deeper. Both of them groaned then Toby rose up on his knees before lowering slowly. They rocked together, fitting as though they were meant to be.

As Toby undulated over him, Jensen watched his lover fall apart because of him. Toby dropped his head and shouted as he came without Jensen touching his cock at all. A few more thrusts and Jensen filled Toby's ass with his cum, more being milked from him as Toby's passage clenched and unclenched around him.

"Toby," he cried out, keeping Toby tight to him as he climaxed.

Finally, Toby collapsed on top of him and he grimaced at the sticky mess between them. Toby chuckled, but didn't move.

"I got a towel," Jensen told him. "It's on the nightstand if you can reach it."

Toby whined when Jensen's softened cock slid from him along with some of his cum to coat his thighs. Then he gathered up the towel to clean them off. Jensen stayed where he was, letting Toby take care of him. Once he was done, Toby tossed the towel in the general direction of their bathroom then tucked a pillow under Jensen's leg before snuggling close to him.

"I missed that," Toby confessed.

Jensen placed a kiss on the top of Toby's head. "So did I. Maybe in the morning, you can do me. I should be all right if I'm on my side."

"Sounds like a plan." Toby traced circles around Jensen's nipples. "You do realize that once we have kids, we probably won't have as much time to make love as we do now. I mean, Coop's pretty self-sufficient once we got the dog door put in."

"I love having that. At least we don't have to let him out at night if he has to go." Jensen grunted when Toby pinched one of his hard nubs. "What was that for?"

"You're so lazy. What if we end up adopting a baby? Are you going to make me be the one who gets up for the late night feedings?" Toby propped his chin on his fist to stare up at Jensen.

Jensen smirked. "I think that's a good idea. You can be our Asian markets expert, so you'd be up anyway. You can give him his late night feedings while making us money."

He yelped when Toby pinched him again, this time harder. Holding his hands up, he laughed.

"I was just kidding. Of course, I wouldn't make you do it all on your own. We're partners in everything. If we didn't have the dog door and Coop needed to go out, I'd take him outside. I'm not afraid of a little work, Toby."

Toby took his hand then placed a kiss on one of the red scars running across his palm. It was where the rope had cut through his gloves and his flesh during his fall. The doctors told him they'd always be there, just faded over time.

"They're kind of ugly, aren't they?" He studied them, yet he didn't hate them. Not like he hated the needle scars on his arms.

"No, they aren't ugly to me," Toby said, kissing it again.

The scars on Jensen's hands spoke to Jensen of courage to face his fears and conquer new places. They showed that he could achieve what he dreamt. The ones on his arms were symbols of his weakness, of his inability to face the world and take it head-on.

Then the flash of his gold band caught his eye and his heart leaped. Of all the scars, tattoos and other things he wore on his body, his wedding ring was the more important because it spoke of love, the one thing no human being could live without and the one thing that was hardest to gain.

Chapter Twenty

*Once the realization is accepted that even between the
closest human beings infinite distances continue, a
wonderful living side by side can grow, if they succeed in
loving the distance between them which makes it possible to
see the other whole against the sky.*

— Rainer Maria Rilke

"I can't believe you actually are taking me cage diving
with Great Whites," Toby exclaimed, as they entered
their room at the South African resort Jensen had
booked for them.

Jensen sat in one of the chairs, grimacing a little while
he rubbed his thigh. "I thought you might like it as an
anniversary present, even if it's a month late."

Toby set his carry-on down then knelt next to Jensen,
taking over the massage. "Are you okay? We should've
taken a golf cart instead of walking from the lobby."

"I'm fine. Just from all the walking and the sitting in
the plane for hours, it's a little stiff." Jensen caressed

Toby's cheek. "Now that I'm totally healed, I thought we could get away from everything for a while."

Nuzzling into Jensen's touch, he gave him a smile. "I know you weren't too thrilled about the idea when Jigger and I discussed it. I figured I'd never be able to get you out on the water, much less in a cage."

Jensen raised his eyebrows. "You will get me out on the water. I can't promise you that I'll actually get in the cage with you."

"That's all right. You don't have to do it if it makes you uncomfortable." Toby finished with Jensen's thigh before pushing to his feet.

He wandered over to the sliding glass doors that led to their balcony. It overlooked the ocean and in the distance, he could see some islands. There were people wandering the beaches, though it was a little cool to be out right then.

"Isn't this like their winter?" he asked as he got busy unpacking their suitcases.

"Yeah, but the websites for the shark diving tours said the best time to see sharks was between March and September when the water's the clearest. March seemed like a good time to come."

He turned to see Jensen stand then grab his own bag from the floor to bring it over to Toby. Together, they finished getting things put away. Once done, Toby turned to look at Jensen.

"What's on the schedule for the rest of the day?"

Jensen took Toby's hips in his hands before tugging him closer. Bending down, he kissed him for a minute or two. When Jensen ended it, he motioned to the bed.

"Take a nap. Wake up. Make love. Go have dinner. Come back. Make love again. Sleep."

Toby pretended to think about it before he grinned. "Sounds like a good plan to me."

He let Jensen maneuver him to the bed where they fell onto it with a sigh. It was huge and soft, perfect for their tired, jet-lagged bodies. Toby curled into Jensen's side, resting his head on Jensen's shoulder while placing his hand on Jensen's chest so he could feel the man's heart beat. Taking a nap wrapped in his husband's arms sounded wonderful to Toby.

* * * *

Wet heat surrounded Toby's cock and he moaned as a rough hand fondled his balls. He groaned as he opened his eyes, looking down to see Jensen lying between his legs. His gorgeous eyes met Toby's and held a sparkle as he swallowed Toby to the base of his shaft.

"Hmm…what a nice way to wake up," he murmured, threading his fingers through Jensen's hair to cup the back of his head. Toby kept his hold light, not forcing Jensen to do anything he didn't want, but he liked having another connection.

He lifted his hips to push into Jensen's mouth and Jensen played with Toby while applying suction. Shuddering, he let his eyes drift closed and allowed pleasure to sweep over him. Toby spread his legs more, then drew his left knee up, exposing his hole. Jensen took the hint and rubbed his thumb over Toby's opening, but didn't press in.

"Come on, Jensen," he begged, wiggling his butt to get Jensen to do more.

Jensen pulled off him with a wet pop then shifted so he rocked back on his heels. "No. I want you to fuck me." After leaning forward, he kissed Toby and wrapped his arms around Toby's shoulder. Then with a sudden movement, he rolled them so he was on the bottom and Toby lay on top of him.

"I'll need to get you ready," Toby cautioned before he allowed Jensen to take him in.

Shaking his head, Jensen motioned to the tube of lube on the top of the blankets. "I got myself ready before I woke you up. I didn't want to waste any time once you were awake."

Toby grabbed the slick then squirted some into his palm to coat his cock. Once that was done, he pushed inside Jensen, going slow but not stopping until he was buried all the way. He braced his hands on either side of Jensen's head and stared into his husband's eyes. Jensen took a deep breath as his body adjusted to being filled.

Jensen took Toby's face in his hands then brought him down to touch their lips together. Then, with only inches between them, he said, "You can move. Please fuck me."

Toby crushed his mouth to Jensen and began to slide out before slamming back in. He knew Jensen didn't need gentle or cautious. Jensen liked the ache of knowing Toby'd been inside him for a day or two afterward.

"Christ!" Jensen shouted when Toby hit his gland on one of his thrusts.

"Right there." Toby grinned as he tried to make sure he worked that spot every time, wanting to drive Jensen out of his mind.

Soon their bodies moved together in a familiar dance. Moans and groans filled the room around them, along with the scent of sex and sweat.

Jensen babbled, "Harder. Faster. Toby, please."

Toby did as he was asked. Snapping his hips, he filled Jensen as deeply as he could. "Touch yourself," he ordered Jensen.

He rose a little so Jensen could wrap his hand around his cock, pumping in time with Toby's strokes. Jensen dropped his head back and a long low moan issued from his throat as he came, covering his hand and stomach with strings of pearly cum.

"Holy shit!" His eyes crossed when Jensen's inner passage clamped down around his length, almost demanding his climax.

Toby came, flooding Jensen's ass while trembling and shouting. He twitched and shuddered, trying to hold himself up so he didn't squash Jensen, but it was as though the muscles in his arms suddenly went limp.

"Omph," Jensen gasped when Toby flopped down on him.

"Sorry. I'll get off you as soon as my body is working again," Toby promised.

Jensen ran his hand down Toby's back to pat his butt cheek. "No problem, love. We can stay like this for a while, though we might be stuck together when we decide to move."

Toby murmured something that he didn't even understand. His eyes drifted shut as he worked to calm his breathing.

His eyes popped open when he was unceremoniously dumped on his back. "Hey," he exclaimed, pushing up on his elbows to watch Jensen wander toward the bathroom. Lying back down on the mattress, he stared up at the ceiling and heard the water running.

"Come in here and clean up," Jensen called out to him.

Sighing, he climbed out before strolling over to join Jensen in the shower. They washed quickly then dried off. After changing into clean clothes, Toby made sure he had his wallet, phone and the hotel key before he motioned for Jensen to head out.

"Lead the way. I'm starving," he told Jensen as they left the room.

"The restaurant here in the hotel is supposed to be good." Jensen rested his hand at the small of Toby's back while they waited for the elevator.

"Sounds good to me." His stomach grumbled and they both laughed.

* * * *

The boat they were on stopped and one of the crew members lowered the anchor. Toby bounced in his seat, excitement rushing through him. He grabbed a hold of Jensen's hand.

"I can't believe we're going to do this."

Jensen shot him an unhappy glance before turning back to watch the water. "You wanted to do it, so I thought we should before the kids come. We won't be taking these kind of trips often after that."

"Nope. We'll be heading to Disney and Legoland." Toby grinned. "Which would be as awesome as this—just different."

"*Oi*, you gentlemen married?" The dive captain asked as he went about getting the cage ready to drop.

"Yes," Toby said slowly, not sure how the man would react. He didn't want to get his ass kicked in the middle of shark-infested waters, but he wasn't going to lie to keep himself safe.

"Good on you, mate." Rusty grinned at them. "Spent a couple of weeks in Hawaii to stand as best man for a couple mates of mine. Got some surfing in as well."

"What's an Australian guy doing in South Africa?" Jensen relaxed, keeping his hold on Toby.

Rusty chuckled as he unhooked the ropes holding the cage on to the back deck of the boat. "The sharks and the surf. Why else would I leave my home?"

"Right." Toby caught Jensen's gaze and smiled. "Sounds like you're a little obsessed."

"There's nothing better than the sea." Rusty waved his hand out over the clear blue expanse surrounding them. "Beauty. Power. Danger. Everything a man could want is out here just waiting for us to find it."

Toby nudged Jensen with his elbow before meeting Rusty's gaze. "I know a man who feels that way about climbing."

Rusty turned to study Jensen. "You climb? Rocks or mountains?"

"Mountains, though I won't be doing that anymore. Probably start doing some more rock climbing now." Jensen touched the bottom of the scar peeking out from the bottom of his swim trunks. "Broke my leg descending to Base Camp on K2. I'd already told Toby I wouldn't be doing more of the big ones, but that kind of sealed the deal for me."

Toby saw Rusty start lifting the hem of the T-shirt he wore. When it had gotten to the height of his chest, Toby gasped at the large scar starting at just under Rusty's armpit to disappear below the waistband of his shorts. It wasn't pretty or smooth. The scar was jagged and looked as though it had been extremely painful.

"Got bit by a tiger shark off the coast of California while I was surfing there. Got over a thousand stitches and lost so much blood, they weren't sure I'd live." Rusty stared at his scars with a fond expression on his face then touched the small tattoo of a Great White that seemed to float on his hip. "Friends thought I was crazy for getting back in the water afterward, but there's nothing else I love more."

"You weren't scared?" Toby asked.

Rusty shook his head. "Nah. Odds are, it's going to happen again if I keep surfing or doing this cage diving gig. While in the ocean, I'm the low man on the totem pole sort to speak. Not only are there sharks, but there are other creatures that could kill me just as easily. I'm just not comfortable anywhere else in the world."

"Rusty, you can get the cage in then start chumming the waters," the captain said from the cabin doorway.

"Yes, sir." Rusty saluted him smartly before turning to work with one of the other crew to get the cage into the ocean.

Jensen leaned into Toby's side and whispered, "That's a stronger obsession than I ever had. Well, except for you."

He nodded, brushing his cheek against Jensen's. "Obsession can be a good thing sometimes though. If he didn't have that, he might never have gotten over that shark attack. Rusty might not ever have gone back to the water without it."

"True."

They were intrigued by the routine the crew had to get everything ready for the dive. It was obvious they'd done it enough times to have it down to an art. The cage floated off the back of the boat, close enough for Jensen and Toby to slip into it without having to swim outside it.

Rusty grabbed a couple of buckets then dumped them over the edge. "This is a special formula the Cap's come up with to draw the sharks in. It works. We'll only have to wait for a little bit before they start coming around."

"How many will come?" Jensen sounded nervous and Toby patted his knee.

Shrugging, Rusty pursed his lips while he stared at the horizon. "Hard to say, but we'll at least get one to show up and that's all you need, right?"

"One would be nice." Jensen's voice wobbled slightly.

"Yeah. We don't need a lot of them. One small shark would be enough for me to be able to brag that I swam with sharks." Toby winked at Rusty, who grinned back at him.

"Well, I guarantee they aren't going to be small. Probably the smallest will be around ten feet." Rusty strolled over the gently rocking deck to them.

"What's the biggest one you've seen?" Toby probably shouldn't have been asking, for Jensen's sanity at the very least, but he was curious.

Rusty pulled out wet suits for them, plus snorkels and fins. While he did that, he spoke, "Hmm...biggest one I've ever seen was an eighteen footer that swam under while I was surfing in Hawaii. She could've cut me and my board right in half with one bite, but she wasn't interested in me at all—just cruised away into the gloom. Nearly wet myself that time."

They got ready and Rusty gave them tips on using the snorkel. Also, warned them to keep their hands inside the cage at all times.

"Easy to get one of them snapped off like a twig by one of these." Rusty tipped his head to the side of the boat and Toby scrambled over to see a large dorsal fin cut through the surface.

The water was so clear that Toby saw the massive torpedo-shaped shark swimming by. It was half as big as the boat and it had to be well over a thousand pounds. He heard a click and turned to see Jensen snapping pictures.

His husband shrugged. "I might not be happy about being out here, but I'm not going to pass up the chance to get photos while we were doing it. We'll pick out our favorite and hang it on the wall with my Everest and K2 pictures."

"Awesome." Toby couldn't wait to get in the water. He wanted to see what they were like up, close and personal.

"All right, mates. Looks like the main attractions are starting to arrive. Which of you wants to go first?" Rusty chuckled when Toby held his hand up. "I figured you'd want to be first. You want the camera? Or you going to trust your man to get some good shots when he's in there?"

He didn't hesitate. "I trust him. He's good at taking pictures."

"All right. Let's get in there then." Rusty helped Toby onto the platform the cage was attached to then into the steel rectangular box that would protect him from the sharks circling the boat.

Two more had arrived while they were settling into the water and Toby gave a silent gasp when one bumped its nose into the steel bars in front of him. Its teeth were jagged rows of serrated triangles and its eyes were black and rather empty, as though it saw Toby as nothing more than a possible meal.

Another rubbed its side along the edge and the cage wobbled precariously. Toby glanced over to Rusty, who just gave him a thumbs up. Obviously nothing was wrong or Rusty would be getting Toby out of there.

He forced himself to relax and began to enjoy being immersed in a world where he couldn't really do anything except accept what went on around him. It was nature at her most deadly and most beautiful.

While being in the ocean and watching the sharks swim around him, Toby began to get a glimpse of how Jensen felt about climbing mountains and how, in many ways, it made him feel small versus the universe that encompassed him. He thought about Jensen who waited above the surface for him, loving him more than he ever had before.

Chapter Twenty-One

*The family you come from isn't as important as the family
you're going to have.*

— Ring Lardner

"Hey Jensen," Toby shouted from the front of the
house.

"Yeah?" Jensen yelled back as he stood staring into
the refrigerator. They needed to go grocery shopping
soon because the cupboards were getting pretty bare.

They hadn't had time to do anything once they got
back from their trip. They'd been working on building
up their clients' portfolios, and looking for the right
adoption agency to work with.

Toby had been excited, but now that the possibility
truly existed for them to adopt a child, Jensen was
getting nervous. Not necessarily second thoughts.
Mostly panicked 'I'm not sure I can do this' thoughts.

What did he know about raising kids or being part of
a family? He certainly didn't have shining examples
when he was growing up. Yet Toby did, so he could

count on his husband to know the right — and wrong — way to do things.

"I need you," Toby called and Jensen shut the door before heading toward the front.

"Do you need help untying your shoes again? I told you double knots are a pain in the ass to get undone," he joked as he walked into the living room then stopped dead in his tracks.

Toby stood, his back to Jensen, yet Jensen had a suspicious feeling he was scowling at the couple that sat on the couch. If the stiffness of Toby's spine didn't give away his unhappiness, the way Coop stood at attention by Toby's feet did.

"Coop, go lie down," Jensen ordered the dog.

Coop looked up at Toby and whined. After bending, Toby rubbed Coop's ears. "Go on. We'll be all right."

Appeased, the dog came over to Jensen to get a pat before he trotted down the hallway toward the kitchen.

"Mother. Father." Jensen moved to stand next to Toby. Shock roiled inside him at the sight of his up until now absent parents. His muscles tightened with tension. "What are you doing here?"

His father stood then offered Jensen his hand. "Jensen. Son. You're looking well."

Toby snorted and Jensen coughed to cover his laughter. *Christ!* Toby had just met them and he seemed to have taken an instant dislike to them.

Jensen shook his hand. "Father. I can't say the same for you."

The years of heavy drinking had taken their toll on Martin Brockhoff, leaving heavy lines on his forehead and around his mouth. Broken blood vessels had turned his nose red and dark smudges underlined his eyes. Vestiges of his younger, more handsome, self remained in the full head of dark hair and the rather trim figure his father still had.

"Mother." Jensen turned to face her. "You're looking much like I remembered you."

Which wasn't shocking, considering how good plastic surgeons were nowadays. Linda Brockhoff's skin was still wrinkle-free and he imagined Botox'd to the hilt, though he wouldn't have been able to tell by her lack of expression. Unless she was angry, his mother wore a blank expression. She'd said it was to stop the wrinkles from happening, but Jensen decided it was because, unless it had to do with spending money or partying, his mother didn't have a thought in her brain.

She inclined her head as though she were the queen acknowledging a subject. "Jensen."

"Why are you here?"

His mother turned her empty gaze to Toby. "Why, to meet your husband, of course. I wonder why we weren't invited to the wedding."

"Because I didn't know where you were and I didn't want you there." There was no point in lying. It wasn't as if it was going to hurt their feelings. Toby encircled his waist, lending support.

His father paled, seemingly appalled by Jensen's comment. He pressed his hand to his heart. "I can't believe you wouldn't want your own parents there on the most important day of your life."

It was Jensen who snorted this time. "You couldn't be bothered to come to any of the other important days in my life. Why would I think you'd want to come to this one?"

"Not come? What are you talking about?" Linda glared at him.

"You didn't come to any of my graduations. Once you shipped me off to boarding school, I never got a card — or any kind of acknowledgement — on my birthday. You were too busy flying around the world or drinking yourself unconscious to think about me." He had to think about not yelling as his own anger began to rise.

His father had the decency to flush, but his mother continued to appear as if she could care less.

"You were an independent child. You never wanted us around to hold your hand or give you hugs." Linda huffed slightly, crossing her arms under her ample chest. "You never allowed me to be your mother."

"That's bullshit!" Jensen took a step toward her, wanting to grab her and shake her until she admitted she was a crappy mother. "You couldn't be bothered by me. All you wanted to do was go out and party with your friends. You left me behind with nannies and the housekeepers. You complained about how being pregnant with me ruined your figure."

Linda shrugged. "It did. Why should I be happy about that?"

"Jensen, we didn't come to rehash past issues," Martin said, holding his hand out grasp Jensen's arm.

Taking one step to the side, Jensen avoided his father's touch. Toby eased between them and Jensen flashed him a grateful smile.

"May I get you a drink?" Toby offered.

Jensen wanted to protest, telling Toby that his parents weren't going to be staying that long, but he bit his tongue again. Clenching his hands together, he let Toby play the gracious host. To be honest, as angry as he was with his parents, it didn't hurt him to treat them well. He could be a better person then they were.

"I'd love a scotch with light ice," Martin told Toby.

"Just water will be fine for me, unless you have some good white wine." Linda didn't appear convinced they would have her quality of alcohol.

Toby shook his head. "I'm sorry. We don't drink. I can offer you coffee, tea or lemonade."

Shock registered on his parents' faces.

"I was an alcoholic by the time I was sixteen," Jensen told them. "I learned from the best, Father. I finally managed to sober up almost eight years ago. It took me longer to get off the drugs."

"So no, we don't have any alcohol in the house," Toby said again.

Martin dropped to sit next to Linda then scrubbed his hands over his face. "I'll have coffee, black. Please."

"I don't suppose you have sparkling water." Her tone spoke of just how annoyed she was about the whole situation.

"No, ma'am. I'll be right back." Toby kissed Jensen on the cheek before he left.

Jensen stood there, staring at his parents for a few tense minutes then said, "Why are you here? I know it's not because you want to reconnect with me after all these years. It's not like I've hidden from you."

"We've always known where you were, even when you lost your mind and left your job to go climb mountains." Linda curled up the corner of her mouth in a sneer. "What were you thinking? You can't make money that way. In fact, you're throwing money away."

Martin threw his wife a disgusted glance. "I've always kept tabs on you, Jensen. Then when you filed paperwork to change your last name, I had to come and see why."

Jensen raised his eyebrows at that statement. "It's been over a year since I got married and did that. If you really wanted to know, why didn't you come right then?"

"We were busy." Linda dismissed Jensen's question with a wave of her hand.

"That doesn't surprise me. One thing that does make me wonder a little is what are you *both* doing here. Last I knew you were living separate lives and weren't even in the same country."

Linda looked at Martin, as though she were telling him it was up to him what explanation he gave. Jensen waited, knowing that whatever had brought his parents to his home was probably going to raise his blood pressure.

"Here we go." Toby walked back in, carrying a tray with coffee and water on it. There were also two glasses of lemonade as well, which Jensen knew were for him and Toby.

After handing Martin and Linda their drinks, Toby motioned for Jensen to sit in one of the chairs across from the couch then brought his lemonade over to him. When he took it, Toby caressed his fingers, again letting him know he wasn't alone in this clusterfuck.

They sat there, staring at each other, until Linda blew out a loud sigh. She set her glass on the coffee table then met Jensen's gaze.

"Your father is a terrible money manager. Somehow he managed to lose a great deal of our fortune during the economic downturn." She glared at Martin.

"You're here for money?" Jensen laughed. "I should've known."

"We don't want your money. We want the money in your trust fund, since it was your father's to begin with." Linda leaned back, a weird expression on her face as though she were trying to smile, but the Botox in her cheeks wouldn't let her.

Jensen shuddered at how doll-like she looked. There was so much plastic in her that she would probably melt if she were caught in a fire. "My trust fund?"

Martin cleared his throat, looking uncomfortable about the entire topic. A little part of Jensen wondered if his father really wanted to be there.

"Yes. I set it up when you were born. You get control of it when you turn thirty-five. I'm not sure why my lawyers haven't contacted you about it before this." Martin frowned.

Narrowing his eyes, Jensen said, "Why don't you just break it, since you're the one who set it up?"

"Because your father's lawyers ensured that it couldn't be broken without a great deal of paperwork and money spent on doing it." Linda examined her fingernails. "Plus, we never thought we'd need it. I went to talk to the people who manage it for you, but they wouldn't tell me anything. Said that since I wasn't on the legal documents, I had no right to know anything about it."

"Were you thinking you'd just take a little bit of the interest? That no one would care and I wouldn't know about it," Jensen asked.

Her hazel eyes, so much like his, met his gaze. "It's *our* money. We put it in there to help you out, but obviously you don't need it." She gestured to the room around them. "It's only right that you give it back to us."

Toby chuckled. "What makes you think it's not my money we're using for all of this?"

Linda looked Toby over from his feet to his head then snorted. "You, honey, aren't the kind of genius with money that my son is. You might be doing all right, but you can't afford all of this, plus all those trips, if my son weren't paying for half of it."

Jensen shared a grin with Toby, but they didn't disillusion her about where the money was coming from. They'd combined their accounts as soon as Jensen got out of the hospital after K2. Plus, Toby actually was better with finances then Jensen was.

It was time to end the charade. He pushed to his feet then propped his fists on his hips as he stared down at his parents. Anger and disappointment swelled in him. He was man enough to admit that when he'd walked into the living room and saw them standing there, he had an unrealistic hope that they were there to reconcile. He should've known better.

"I can't do this anymore."

Everyone turned to look at him. Toby's expression merely held interest and he felt a surge of confidence, knowing that Toby trusted him not to do something stupid. His father bit his lip, worry and a certain amount of embarrassment showing on his face. His mother dropped her gaze to focus intently on her shoes.

"I know all about the trust fund." He turned to Toby. "I was going to talk to you tonight since we'd gotten done with work early. The lawyers sent a letter while we were in South Africa and I just called them earlier this afternoon."

Toby held up his hand. "Jensen, don't worry. I know you would've told me when you had the chance."

He faced his parents again. "I know exactly how much is in the trust fund and that I'll get complete control of it next year. I'm not interested in helping you."

Linda squawked and Martin nodded, as though he had expected it. Jensen shook his head at his mother to keep her from speaking.

"Maybe if you had shown any kind of interest — or love — for me, I'd be more willing to help you, but you both tossed me aside as though I was an inconvenience in your lives." Jensen went to Toby and after taking his hand, he pulled Toby to his feet. He wrapped his arm around Toby's waist before tugging him close. "Toby has never shown me anything except love and acceptance, even after I nearly screwed the whole thing up. He's made me a part of his family, and they love me without me having to do anything to earn it."

"We love you, don't we, Martin?" Linda poked her husband. "If we didn't, we wouldn't have set up that trust for you."

"Money doesn't equate with love, Mom. At least not to me. You can leave." He pointed to the front door.

Toby cupped his face with his hands then lowered it to whisper a kiss over his lips. "Go start making a list of what we need from the grocery store. I'll see your parents out then we can go shopping and grab something to eat as well."

After nodding, Jensen walked back to the kitchen and continued on to the deck where he dropped into one of the lounge chairs. He leaned his head back to rest on the cushion while he closed his eyes. He slowly inhaled and exhaled a couple of times, working on calming down.

A cold nose nudged his hand, causing him to look down and spot Coop sitting next to him. He grinned as he rubbed the dog's ears. "Families suck, Coop, but something tells me you might already know that."

He traced one of the scars that ran the length of Coop's side. The dog whined and wiggled, clearly enjoying the attention Jensen was paying him. After standing, Jensen went to grab the tennis ball Coop loved to fetch. He didn't know how long they played before Toby came outside to find him.

"They gone?" He didn't look at Toby, just kept throwing the ball for Coop.

Toby slipped his arms around Jensen, letting him lean back against him. He nuzzled Jensen's neck. "Yes. I gave them the name of our lawyers and told them that all communication must go through them until you change your mind...if you ever do."

Rolling his eyes, Jensen doubted he'd ever try to talk to them again. Coming to ask him for money was another shining example of why they had no idea just how terrible of parents they'd been.

"Are you disappointed in me?" he asked softly.

Toby stiffened then eased far enough away that he could turn Jensen around so they faced each other. When their gazes met, Toby inquired, "Why would I be disappointed in you?"

Clearing his throat, he fidgeted a little bit before saying, "Because I didn't help them out."

"Why would you do that? They've never really helped you out." Toby paused for a second. "Maybe they helped with college, but other than that, they've never done anything for you. Why should you go out of your way to help them? It's *their* fault, not yours."

A sudden thought hit Jensen. "You're right. Dad did pay for college. What do you think of me repaying him for my education? There's more than enough in the fund to cover that."

Toby watched Coop sniff around the edges of the backyard for a few minutes while he seemed to be thinking. "I think that's a great idea. It shows you're being the bigger person, but you're not letting them push you over either. What are you going to do with the rest of it?"

Jensen smiled. "I'm going to let it continue earning interest and we're going to use it as an education fund for our children. This way they can go—or do—anything they want without having to worry about how to pay for it."

"Brilliant idea." Toby smacked his ass before go back inside to the kitchen. "Come on. We need food, man, and I'm starving."

Jensen whistled Coop to him then they followed Toby. He remained quiet for a while as Toby got a list together of food before they set out to the store. Finally, when they were in the car and on their way home, Toby twisted in his seat to face Jensen.

"What's your problem? You've said hardly two words since we left the house. Are you still worried about your parents? I told you they won't bother us again. If you want, I can have our lawyers talk to them and impress upon them the importance of obeying our wishes." Toby wrapped his hand around Jensen's biceps.

He shook his head. "No. I'm not thinking about that. I'm just remembering all the times I tried so hard to get one of them to acknowledge me. All the things I did to make them proud. None of it mattered. Hell, they don't care that I climbed Everest and K2, if they even know that I accomplished that. All they're interested in is the money. It's always been that way."

"Well," Toby hedged a little. "You know I do think your father might be embarrassed about the whole thing. He did seem upset when your mother pushed it."

Laughing, Jensen explained, "He was embarrassed and upset that he wasn't the one who manipulated me into giving them all of the money. He never liked it when Mother overstepped her boundaries and spoke about things that didn't concern a woman."

"Money isn't a woman's place?" Toby laughed. "Tell that to my mom. She has complete control of the checkbook. Dad goes to her when he wants to buy something and she has to give him permission."

"We've already established your family is very different from mine," Jensen commented, though he did smile at the image of gruff Donald having to plead with his wife for spending money.

Toby nodded. "True. Do you really think that there's no possibility of you reconciling with them?"

Jensen pulled into their driveway. "Not now. I stopped loving them a long time ago. Now I married into a great family and I couldn't be happier."

"Good. Keep those happy thoughts when I tell you that they're all coming for a visit next weekend, along with the kids." Toby winked as Jensen groaned.

But he didn't care. Not really. He loved how loud and rowdy the children—and adults—of the Schwartzel family could be. He adored how Nancy always gave him a huge hug and kiss. Donald would clap his back and ask about different sports teams.

They'd taken him in without question, once Toby had told them about loving him. He'd never had a choice in the matter, and Jensen had wanted it that way. He wasn't going to look a gift horse in the mouth, not after all the stupid shit he'd done. The universe had smiled down on him the day he met Toby. Jensen would always be grateful for that.

Chapter Twenty-Two

There is only one happiness in this life, to love and be loved.

– George Sand

"Is there anything you don't want?" Vanessa, the adoption agency representative, peered over her half glasses at them.

Toby frowned and shot a quick glance at Jensen. "What do you mean?"

"I mean are you only interested in babies? Only want white children? Only boys?" She tapped her fingernails on her desk while waiting for an answer.

"Oh my God, people really have those qualifications on their adoption searches?" Toby was horrified that people wouldn't be willing to give any kid who needed it a place to grow up loved and wanted.

Vanessa shrugged. "Yes." While she didn't say anything, her opinion on those people was obvious in the curled lip.

Jensen shook his head. "No. We have no restrictions. We're looking for kids who need love and a home. If we meet one that we think we wouldn't be good for, we'll let you know."

"So you don't have a problem with handicaps or illnesses?" Vanessa typed away.

"No." Toby took Jensen's hand in his. "If it turns out that the child we want to adopt is in a wheelchair or needs special things, we're more than willing to provide those things for them."

She smiled at him. "With that attitude, we should be able to find you some prospective children soon. It's the couples who come in here with very specific ideas on the child they wish to have that make my job difficult." Her eyes lit up. "In fact, I think I might have just the kid. He's been in the foster system for about three years now. His mother died and his father wasn't around. No one in his blood family wanted him."

"Does he have any issues that we should know about before we meet him? I want to make sure we're prepared for it."

Vanessa laughed. "Actually, there's nothing wrong with Dante. He's developmentally delayed. It comes from not have the proper nutrition while in the womb and for the first two years of his life. I talked to the therapists who have worked with him, and they swear he'll catch up eventually. He just needs a chance and a forever home. He's been in the same foster home for six months now, so there's been stability of a sort there."

"And they don't want to adopt him?" He couldn't see opening his house to a child, taking care of him and loving him then letting him go, even if the other family he was going to would keep him forever.

"No. They have three kids of their own and while they have no problem fostering a child, they don't want to adopt one." Vanessa didn't seem upset, so Toby imagined a lot of the foster families were like that.

"All right. We'd love to meet him. How does this work?" Jensen said, nodding at Toby.

Vanessa stood then wandered over to a cabinet. After pulling out a file, she brought it over to them. "Here's Dante's file. It'll fill you in on his background and health while I give his caseworker a call. We can set up a meeting—maybe at a park or the zoo. Some place he'll have fun and not feel uncomfortable."

Toby and Jensen edged closer to each other so they could go over the file together. Toby's eyes filled when he saw Dante's picture clipped to the first page. "Oh, he's adorable."

"He is. Says his mother was Jamaican and his father was from Georgia," Jensen read from the file. "I wonder how they met and why did his father leave?"

"We'll never know. All effort was made to contact the man, but it's like he just disappeared. It's possible to go off the grid completely if you really want to," Vanessa informed them.

"It says he'll be starting kindergarten in the fall."

Vanessa nodded. "Yes. He completed pre-school and his teacher thought he was a well-behaved child. Well...as behaved as a five year old can be. He's already beginning to catch up to his peers. It'll just take a little more work on your part."

"That would be fine. We own a small investment firm, so it wouldn't be a big deal for us to take time off as needed." Excitement rushed through Toby. He couldn't wait to meet Dante. He just had a strange feeling that they would all hit it off and Dante would make the perfect fit with Jensen and him.

"Wonderful. Like I said, I'll call his caseworker and see what we can set up for you to meet Dante. Then I'll call you with the arrangements. It might take a day or two," she warned them.

Jensen pushed to his feet then brought Toby up to his. He held out his hand. "Thank you so much for all your help."

Vanessa took his hand in hers then covered it with her other. "You seem like a loving couple, Mr. Schwartzel, and Dante is a young boy who has a special place in my heart. When I looked over your application, I had a feeling you might be the perfect parents for Dante."

"Will us being a gay couple make any difference?" Toby knew it wasn't supposed to, but he couldn't help asking.

"No. Who you're married to makes no difference here. All that matters is that you pass all the qualifications and tests, which you have." Vanessa beamed at both of them. "I think you'll be marvelous parents, no matter which child you end up adopting."

After they walked out of the agency's building, Toby whirled around then threw his arms around Jensen's neck. He hugged him hard before pressing a loud kiss to his lips.

"We're going to be fathers," he exclaimed, almost giddy with happiness.

Jensen hugged him back then released him. "Don't get your hopes up too high about Dante. He sounds like a great kid, but who knows? We might not hit it off when we meet. He has to like us as well, Toby."

Toby nodded. "I know. It's just I have this feeling that Dante's the one — or the first of at least two."

"We never did discuss how many we wanted," Jensen replied, offering his arm to Toby and waiting for him to take it before they strolled down the street toward the garage where they'd parked their car.

Toby thought about for a little bit while they walked. Then he shrugged. "I don't think I have a definite number. Let's see how it goes with Dante — or whoever we end up with—before we jump the gun to adopt another."

Chuckling, Jensen agreed. "Yeah. Dante first, then we'll worry about more."

He glanced at his watch. "We need to get home. Simpson and the guys are coming over for dinner and cards tonight. He's bringing steaks to grill, but I told him we'd provide the sides."

"All right."

They got to their vehicle then headed home. Toby couldn't help thinking about Dante and the possibility of meeting him.

* * * *

Toby dropped his phone on his desk then shot to his feet. He wiggled and danced for a moment before dashing across the hall to Jensen's office. His husband glanced up from the computer screen he'd been staring at with intense focus.

"What?"

"Vanessa set up a meet and greet with us and Dante for Wednesday at the park just down the street here. If that goes well, then his caseworker will bring him over to the house on Saturday. We'll be able to spend even more time together then." He shoved Jensen's chair back from the desk then flopped onto Jensen's lap. "We're one step closer to starting our family."

Jensen drew him down to him and their lips met in a slow and easy kiss. Like so often happened, desire flared between them. Toby ran his hands over Jensen's chest, slipping his fingers in between the buttons of his dress shirt to tease the warm skin underneath. Their tongues dueled while he began working off Jensen's tie.

He growled. "Why are you wearing a tie? We don't have any clients coming in today."

"I dress for success," Jensen teased then gently set Toby on the edge of the desk before dashing across the room to lock the door. He whirled around and Toby chuckled when his eyes widened to see that Toby had moved.

Toby had somehow managed to get his pants unbuttoned and pushed down to his knees by the time Jensen was done. He glanced over his shoulder to where Jensen stood.

"Come and fuck me," he ordered, wiggling his ass at him.

Jensen groaned then it was Toby's turn when Jensen's hands landed on his butt with a rough touch. Toby rocked back and moaned, gripping the edge of the desk as tightly as he could.

"I can't believe we're doing this in the middle of the day at our office," Jensen mumbled as he pressed his thumb into Toby.

"I don't see you stopping," Toby pointed out then yelped when Jensen pinched one of his cheeks.

"Good thing you're still stretched from this morning." Jensen stepped up to start pushing his cock into Toby's channel.

Toby sucked in a breath as he tried to relax. "So am I," he croaked. The pressure was incredible, but he didn't fight it, knowing it would be okay once Jensen was inside.

When the cold metal of Jensen's belt buckle rubbed over the back of his thighs, Toby exhaled. Jensen reached around to wrap his hand around Toby's cock. He tightened his grip until Toby whimpered from the pain, but it did take his mind off the burn in his ass.

Letting his head drop so he could rest his forehead against the cool surface of the desk, Toby cleared his throat then said, "You can move now."

"I can, huh? Maybe I want to stay here for a moment and just savor how amazing you feel surrounding me," Jensen whispered against his back. He stroked Toby's length, alternating the rhythm and strength.

"Jensen," Toby whined, twitching and shifting, trying to get Jensen to do something except fill him, though he wasn't really arguing about that.

He moaned when Jensen encircled his waist, pressed his free hand to Toby's chest and lifted him so he was standing. The angle drove Jensen in deeper and Toby clenched around his shaft, drawing a shuddering gasp from Jensen.

"We really can't do anything in this position," Toby reminded him, but Jensen laughed.

"Don't worry about it," Jensen told him then began pumping fast, not giving Toby any chance to catch his breath or relax.

Toby rose up on his toes then dropped back down, crying out as somehow Jensen's cock hit his gland. Yet when he tried it again, Jensen held him still.

"You don't do that. I want you to come first and feel you do it around me." Jensen gave him no quarter when he pressed his thumb into Toby's slit while tugging on Toby's balls.

All the sensations overwhelmed Toby — his cock, his ass and his neck were being manhandled as though Jensen was waging war against him. Yet there was no reason for that because Toby yielded his body, heart and soul to the man he loved. Jensen Schwartzel — his husband.

At that thought, Toby came, spilling his seed over Jensen's hand to splatter on the floor by their shoes. As his climax waved through him, his inner passage massaged Jensen's erection.

Jensen shouted while hot liquid flooded Toby's ass and Toby winced as his softening cock slid from Jensen's hand. He yielded when Jensen pressed his hand to his back, encouraging him to bend over. After folding his arms so he could rest his head on them, he sighed, his energy waning.

He wanted to collapse to the floor and curl up in a ball to take a nap. Jensen patted his butt before shuffling over to the other side of his desk. Watching, Toby chuckled when Jensen pulled some wet wipes out of one of the drawers.

"Where did you get those and why do you have them in your desk?" He narrowed his eyes mockingly. "What do you get up to in here that I don't know about?"

Jensen rolled his eyes as he cleaned off his hands and cock. "It's because we eat our lunch here a lot and I can clean my hands. Also, wipe down the phone and the keyboard and stuff when you're sick."

Toby snorted. "When have you become a germaphobe?"

"It has nothing to do with germs. I just like to make sure it's disinfected." Jensen cleared his throat and Toby laughed.

He fell silent when Jensen came over to clean him up as well. Once that was done, he stood to arrange his clothes.

"Here. Clean up the floor."

Turning just in time to catch the container of wipes that Jensen threw at him, Toby leered at Jensen while he tucked his cock back in his pants then did them up. Jensen ran his hand over his hair and stared at Toby.

"Are you certain you want to start a family with me?"

Toby paused in the middle of throwing away the wipes to look at Jensen. At the doubt in Jensen's eyes, Toby tossed them in the trash before racing over to launch himself in Jensen's arms. He pressed a dozen kisses all over Jensen's face then stepped back.

"I love you so much, Jensen Schwartzel, and, hell yes, I want to start a family with you. You have an amazing amount of love in your heart that needs to be shared. Not just with me, but with family—whether that's our kids or our friends. You broke my heart when you ran away eight years ago, but you returned to heal it, and I realized I never had a choice. I had to take you back because love isn't easily forgotten or changed." Toby wiped a tear from the corner of Jensen's eyes.

"Coming back to you was the smartest thing I've ever done," Jensen admitted. He swept Toby in his arms, crushing him to his chest. "I love you, Toby, and I'll adore all the children we will have."

Toby laid his head on Jensen's chest. "It doesn't matter if we get Dante—or not. As long as we have each other and our family, we'll have a pretty good life."

Jensen rubbed his cheek over Toby's head and murmured his agreement. Toby absorbed Jensen's warmth, knowing that they would have to get back to work soon, but taking the time to hold his husband made the idea of the rest of the day brighter.

"Come on. We need to get things taken care of, so we can go start the rest of our life together."

Toby grinned when Jensen said that. As he left Jensen's office, he thought about everything that had gone on in their relationship. He understood that he would love Jensen, no matter where he traveled in the world and how many mountains he climbed because they were stronger with each other than any obstacle the world could throw at them.

About the Author

There is beauty in every kind of love, so why not live a life without boundaries? Experiencing everything the world offers fascinates T.A. and writing about the things that make each of us unique is how she shares those insights. When not writing, T.A.'s watching movies, reading and living life to the fullest.

T.A. Chase loves to hear from readers. You can find her contact information, website and author biography at http://www.pride-publishing.com.

www.ingramcontent.com/pod-product-compliance
Lightning Source LLC
Chambersburg PA
CBHW030142180626
46812CB00002B/814